YELLOW JACK AND TURPENTINE

YELLOW JACK AND TURPENTINE

Mara W. Cohen Ioannides

Contents

Dedication   viii

1	Acknowledgements	1
2	Forward	2
3	The Leaving	4
4	The Departure	12
5	The Crossing	22
6	The Embarkation	27
7	The Reunion	32
8	A New Beginning	42
9	The Adventure	59
10	The Countryside	73
11	The New Day	79
12	The Home Coming	83
13	The Spring	86
14	The Rains	94
15	The Fever	98
16	The Recovery	103
17	The Store	108

18	The Boys' Failure	111
19	The Cabin	119
20	The Farm	124
21	The Tree	129
22	The Fever Returns	131
23	The End	135
24	The Letter	139
25	Epilogue	141
26	Notes	145

Copyright © 2024 by Mara Cohen Ioannides

All rights reserved. No part of this book may be reproduced in any manner whatsoever without written permission except in the case of brief quotations embodied in critical articles and reviews.

First Printing, 2024

For my mother
Brenda Helene Cooperman Cohen
who shared with me a love of historical fiction

Acknowledgements

I was assisted by many people along the way: Mary Annette Wardell, my physician and friend, who helped me understand malaria; Merlin Coffee, a dear friend whose father was a physician in the Ozarks, provided insight into medical practices; Robert Still, my uncle, knows pretty much everything about trains in North America; Ellen Eisenberg, a friend and colleague, introduced me to this family through Kate Herder's memoir many years ago and was willing to read a draft and provide information; Cherri Jones, my treasured friend, who always supports my writing, listens willingly, and read a draft of this novel; and Anne Marie Baker, a booklover friend, carefully proofed this book. My husband, Rob Anderson, suggested I write this book and enjoyed as much as I did finding out little tidbits of Ozarks life and wanted it published as much as I do. Each of these people provided just a bit more detail and passion to the pages.

2

Forward

There is much in this story that is true and some that is not. The point of this story is to try to bring back to life a lost piece of American and American Jewish history.

In 1883, one hundred fifty Jews settled in an area outside of Newport, Arkansas. Their plan was to farm. Various philanthropic organizations funded their venture as a way to move poor Russian Jews away from the urban east coast. This group believed they had found Eden in the New World and wrote to friends in New York City about this paradise. Thus, while this story is based on a real experience and many of the characters, both on the commune and in Arkansas, are real people, much has been fictionalized. So is the way of historical fiction. However, this should provide a good feeling for what it was like for these immigrants in the strange world on the edge of the Ozarks in the early 1880s.

> —A colony of about fifty Polish Jews passed up the river on the steamer Winnie on Sunday night. They will locate in Black River township, Independence county.—*Jacksonport Herald*, 24th ult.

News Story About the First Group
"Local News," Batesville Guard, March 7, 1883, page 3.

3

The Leaving

It was May of 1882. Moyshe gathered his family around him: his wife Ruchel, and his daughters Anna, 8, Hannah, 6, and Gittel, 5. In his wife's arms was their baby Saul. Moyshe checked on his friend Mordechai Woskoboynikoff who was with them. He had his wife Sheyndel and sons Hirsch, 8, and Mendel, 4. The two men lifted their children into the back of a wagon and then helped their wives climb in as well. Then they tossed in the bundles and finally climbed over the buckboard and settled in.

Ruchel and Sheyndel covered their children with blankets and straw, hushing them as they did so. Baby Saul started to whimper, and Ruchel loosened her blouse to find a breast to feed him. It was night and the two families wanted to leave Odessa as quietly as possible. They had said their good-byes to family and friends the last two days and now wanted to leave unnoticed.

Once Moyshe was sure everyone was safe and settled, he called out and the driver headed to the train station. The clacking of the horses' hooves on the cobble streets was hypnotic and soon everyone was asleep. Other than the groaning of the wagon and the clacking, was the sound of the *samovar*[1] rattling against the boards. The families had little to take with them on this mad adventure to America, but Ruchel refused to forgo her mother's *samovar*. As she dozed, she realized she would have to wrap it better so that it would not get damaged.

Odessa
Rue Richelieu, Odessa, Russia, i.e., Ukraine, ca. 1890. Library of Congress, www.loc.gov/item/2001697469/.

Samovar
Pavel Pavlovich Khoroshikh, Samovar. Russian Federation Balagansk Irktusk Oblast, 1927. Library of Congress, www.loc.gov/item/2018688001/.

Just as Ruchel rebuttoned her blouse, the wagon stopped at the train station. It was a noisy place filled with Jewish emigrants desperate to get out of Mother Russia after the last pogrom. Moyshe and Mordechai wiped the sleep from their eyes and climbed out of the wagon. The men were well aware of the pogrom survivors but did not stare. Most survivors came with a small bundle. Many wore bandages to cover wounds. Some were missing limbs. They all had the same blank, scared look on their faces. It was clear they were emotionally exhausted. The women first handed down the bundles that would be their luggage. Then they handed the children. Hannah, Anna, and Hirsch were awake now, though exhausted. They stood quietly hand-in-hand next to the bundles. Gittel and Mendel would not wake up, so Moyshe held them both while Mordechai helped their wives down. Then the children and bundles were parceled out and the two men lead their families through the station to the train headed to Hamburg.

The group was still quiet. The power of the moment, of actually leaving the city, was emotionally overwhelming. Hannah, Gittle, and Hirsch, as young children, saw this whole experience as a grand adventure. Anna understood the weight the adults felt. The adults were almost numb. They were leaving their homeland, their extended families, everything they knew to go somewhere they'd never been. They were scared. They were sad. They were excited.

Odessa Train Station
Odessa Train Station, 1900-1914, Odessa Collection, Romanov Empire, www.romanovempire.org/media/odessa-train-station-1900-1914-461eoc.

Mordechai stopped various station officials asking where to go, and finally the little group found their car in the train. Herding everyone to their seats, the men stayed awake only long enough to hand the conductor their tickets and then, they too succumbed to exhaustion.

In the morning the children sat with their noses stuck against the glass watching the world whiz by. They had no idea how long the ride to Hamburg was, only that it was north and could not even understand what "going to America" really meant.

Ruchel untied one bundle and produced a smaller bundle. After unknotting it, she tried to hand the children some bread and cheese, but the children couldn't be drawn away from the window.

"Children," she cooed in Russian, "Time for eating. The world will be there for a few days." Anna waved her hand behind her head in a dismissive manner at her mother. The others could not even bother with that. They were amazed at the speed of the train and the wonders outside. None of them had been outside the city except on the rare picnic. Thus, the lush green fields and forests just beginning to bloom were amazing.

Ukrainian Landscape
Vasily Polenov, Landscape with River, 1888, www.wikiart.org/en/vasily-polenov/landscape-with-a-river-1888.

Ruchel glared at Sheyndel. Sheyndel grinned, leaned over, and shut the window shade. The five children groaned in union.

"Mamma," Hirsch moaned. "Why did you do that?"

"Did you not hear Mrs. Herder tell you it was time for breakfast?" she asked.

"Uhm...no..."

"Well she did and you all ignored her. I had to get your attention somehow," she replied curtly. "Once you all eat your bread, then I will open the shade."

By this time, Moyshe and Mordechai had woken up. They stretched and yawned and then thanked Ruchel for the bread and cheese. The children gobbled up their food before the adults had gotten four bites swallowed. True to her word, Sheindel reopened the shade and the children gathered around the window once more.

Mordechai swallowed a bite of cheese and turned to his friend. "Do you think we got out in time?" he asked in a hushed tone.

"I'm not sure there is ever a perfect time," responded his companion in equally hushed tones. "But we certainly had to leave. Luckily, our fortune was enough to buy the tickets."

"The 'storms in the *Negev*'[2] have become almost predictable," bemoaned Mordechai. "I was beginning to fear for my wife and boys."

"Living through the first one last year was certainly enough for me," agreed Moyshe through a bite of bread. "The destruction and anger were truly frightening, especially as these were our neighbors rioting."

"Keep your voices down," commanded Ruchel in a whisper. "The children shouldn't be disturbed. They didn't know what was happening and I don't want them to know now."

"Yes, my dear," agreed her husband. "We are off to the Golden Land. Let's focus on the bright future ahead of us."

"The fresh wholesome countryside," said Sheindel wearily. "I've always wanted a little house, not an apartment in a larger house. And windows that look out over fields and gardens, not cobblestones and my neighbors."

"I want to farm," responded Moyshe. "For far too long Jews have been stereotyped as scholars and bookish. It is time we become independent people."

"Yes, dear," Ruchel sighed, "and we will own land and live off the earth. We do not need to be convinced. We are going on this 'adventure', right?"

Sheyndel put her hand on Ruchel's forearm and whispered, "Relax, your husband is only boosting his own courage." Ruchel gently placed her hand over Sheindel's in acknowledgement.

"Be patient, wife," urged Sheyndel's husband. "First we will meet our companions in the city of New York and work to save to buy our farm."

"True, but at least it will be safe and there will be no restrictions. The new laws the czar has instituted against the Jews may seem slight, but who knows where they will lead," answered Moyshe.

"Oh heavens," burst in Ruchel, "I have a cousin who cannot get home to his family because he was in a different village when the law was announced. Now he cannot get a pass to return home."

"What ever will they do?" queried her friend.

"It seems they are considering immigrating to America because that would be easier than bribing government officials to get a pass to return home," sighed Ruchel.

"Who ever heard of such a thing," replied Sheyndel. "Like this is such an easy trip: days on the train, weeks on a ship, and then a whole new country. I wonder what it will be like there?" she asked no one.

And the two couples lapsed into silence. Each pondering their future, as the Russian countryside sped past them.

Days later, they arrived at the Hamburg station. Ruchel strapped baby Saul to her with a shawl so that she could have both hands free. With one she took her bundle and with the other she took Gittel's hand. Anna took Gittel's other hand in hers and her bundle, as large as she was, with her empty hand. In this way, Ruchel struggled to get off the train without tripping over anyone or anyone tripping over her and without losing her girls. Moyshe threw the bundle with the samovar over one shoulder, handed Hannah her bundle and took her free hand. Then he followed his wife down the narrow aisle of the train. Mordechai and Sheyndel followed, each with a boy in tow.

The group wandered the station. Luckily Moyshe was fluent in German, along with their native Russian. He asked various station employees and German police officers where to find their travel company before they were directed in the correct direction. Finally, he got hold of the representative of the steamer company. This man sent them off to an area where there were other emigrants traveling on the same ship. Finally, a young man asked them to follow him a place where they could stay as they awaited the boarding of their ship in a few days. As Moyshe was one of the few who understood German, he worked as a translator for the group. The unmatched, unwashed troupe of travelers carrying bundles and bags and trunks and children followed behind. They gawked at the trams and the police and the well-dressed. Most of the crowd came from *shtetls*[3] that didn't even have paved roads, so they stumbled over the cobbles. Eventually, they came to the hostel where the steamer company would house the crowd for the three days until the ship was ready to leave port. The group settled in the lobby on the inside stairs and even on the outside steps to await their turn to check in.

Horse Drawn Tram
"Station du Tramway, Rue Tiraspolakaja," Odessa, 1900-1914, postcard.

Eventually, Moyshe heard the representative call: "Herder! *Herr*[4] Herder?!"

He gathered his family and followed the path through the people to the representative standing at the desk.

"Here we are," he responded.

"Tickets please," the man said curtly without looking up. Moyshe handed over the tickets. "Ah, steerage. You will find some beds upstairs. The toilets are outside, and we do not serve meals. Your boarding time will be posted on the wall behind me. Safe travels." And he handed back the tickets, after making some marks in his book. He said all this without looking up or even acknowledging that Moyshe and Ruchel were in front of him.

"Kahn! *Frauline*[5] Kahn!" he shouted almost in Moyshe's face.

Totally overwhelmed from the traveling and the newness, Moyshe threw his bundle over his shoulder and headed up the stairs. They wandered the corridor until they found a room with enough beds. Hannah and Anna immediately claimed the upper bunk. Gittel wasn't so sure, but after using the chamber pot, she was too tired to argue when her father sat her on the mattress next to her big sisters. Ruchel tucked their bundles under the bed and in the corners so they would be safe. She laid Saul on the floor on a folded blanket so that she could manage other things.

"Children," she commanded. "Let me see your feet."

Suddenly six feet swung down over the edge of the bed. One by one, Ruchel untied the laces and took the shoes off, dropping them at her feet. As she bent to gather them, the children rolled into their bed and fell asleep.

After removing her dress and stocking, she turned to Moyshe and said, "A bed that is still. I never thought I would relish it so much."

"Well, enjoy, my dear. Our beds, such as they will be on the ship, will never be still." And before he removed his shoes, she was asleep.

4

The Departure

Finally, the day came to board the ship. Ruchel rechecked that everything they owned was packed back in their bundles. After a frantic search of the room, the last spoon was found. Someone had kicked it under a bed, and it was lodged behind the leg.

Sheyndel came into the room wagging her head sadly, "Did you hear? The Pinksies still have wet laundry on the line."

Ruchel responded distractedly, "Well, I guess it gets packed wet. Where is Moyshe? Where are the children?"

Sheyndel put her arm across her friend's shoulder, "Relax, the men, children, and our bags are downstairs. I came up to help you finish and get you downstairs."

Ruchel took a deep breath and released it slowly and loudly. Sheyndel double checked the knots on Ruchel's bundle. They took each other's hands and stared into each other's brown eyes. Sheyndel's were darker, but Ruchel's sparkled more when she smiled. They gave each other a nod of courage. Ruchel grabbed her bundle by the knot at the top and they left the room for their families downstairs.

Downstairs Moyshe had corralled the five children into a corner and had them sit on their bundles. Anna held the baby, who slept peacefully amidst the chaos. Mordechai guarded the group while keeping an eye on the stairwell so their wives would not miss them. Moyshe had gone to find out the details of where they needed to go and what the timetable was.

"Here! Here!" called out Mordechai a bit more anxiously than he had hoped. He really did not want to frighten the children. "There are your mammas. Whoo hoo!! Over here!" he called as loudly as he could and waved his hat over his head. While he could not be heard over the din, Sheyndel did recognize his hat. She determinedly led Ruchel through the crowd to their children.

"Oh my, where's my husband?" cried Ruchel.

Mordechai gently took her bundle from her. "No worries, since Moyshe is the one who can speak German, he went to find out details about how to board the ship."

Ruchel sat down heavily on her bundle. Her *babushka*[6] slipped off her head. Little Gittel came over and tried to pull the *babushka* back up her head but only messed up her mother's hair.

"Little one," Ruchel cooed, "You are an angel." And she pulled the five-year-old close to her in a desperate hug. Then she sat her daughter on her lap, repaired her hair, and returned the *babushka* to its rightful place.

At that moment, Moyshe returned. "Come everyone," he commanded. "We need to get to port and get in line to board our ship to America." Immediately, the children jumped up. Anna impatiently tried to get her mother to take the baby, almost pushing Saul into his mother's arms. Ruchel dutifully took her son as she stood. She grabbed her shawl and quickly turned it into a carrier for the baby. Then she hoisted her bundle onto her shoulder and grabbed Gittel's hand. Anna took her bundle and Gittel's other hand as the group made, almost forced, their way through the crowd.

Port of Hamburg Between 1890 and 1930
Keystone View Company, "General view of the famous German Harbor of Hamburg", Germany. Library of Congress, www.loc.gov/item/2020679997/.

Once outside the hostel with Moyshe in the lead, since he could read the German signs, the two families followed the line of travelers to the port. There they waited not terribly patiently to have their passports scrutinized. Despite the actions of the German immigration officers and the ship company's personnel, disorder was everywhere. Many of those in line were surrounded by families weeping. The agony of the parents as they wished their children, often barely teenagers, a safe and fruitful trip, only made Ruchel clutch Gittel's hand even tighter. The weeping was overwhelming, both the noise and the emotional pain. Then when the time came to release their loved ones so the emigrants could enter the dock and board the ship, the discord became almost unbearable. The ship's crew had to tear mothers and wives from the travelers.

S.S. Fulda
The family actually came on the S.S. Bohemia, but this is an equivalent ship. J.S. Johnston, S.S. Fulda, 1882-1899, Detroit Publishing. Library of Congress, www.loc.gov/item/2016795269/.

Hirsch looked up at his father fearfully. "They won't do that to us?" he asked tearfully.

"No lad, we are travelling together. Those families are leaving some people behind," Mordechai replied gently, trying not to let his son feel his own sadness.

When the two families made it to the boarding area, they found they were forced to wait. There was no shelter from the early summer sun and no place to sit, but despite the complaints of a few, the answer remained the same, "First class boards before steerage." This meant more than just the people, apparently. The children put down their bundles and sat. Ruchel began to nurse Saul as he had been crying in hunger. The crowd watched as trunk after trunk went up the gangway.

Sheyndel turned to her friend, "How can these people need so much? What does one need but a change of clothes and a bowl, cup, and spoon?"

"Don't forget a bed," laughed Ruchel. "But I cannot answer your question. We brought only what we can carry and that is all we need."

"Plus, a *samovar*," laughed Moyshe with a crooked smile. While the *samovar* was unwieldy, he understood his wife's need for it and so didn't complain when she packed it.

Finally, the last trunk went up the gangway and the gate holding back the over one thousand steerage passengers was lifted. The crowd surged forward only to stop again. There were only four shipping agents to check everyone's tickets. A groan of frustration went through the crowd. Some called out in a panic, "Don't let the boat leave without me!" But considering the mixture of languages being spoken by the crowd (Polish, Russian, German, Yiddish, Norwegian, etc.), people only felt the sentiment from the tone rather than understanding the words. Mordechai and Moyshe checked their pockets to make sure their tickets were still there. Sheyndel and Ruchel double checked that their broods were still nearby. Then they settled in to wait yet longer.

They inched even closer to the ship until finally Moyshe was able to hand his ticket to the agent. "Two adults and three children," announced the agent. He didn't look up; he simply waited for an answer.

"*Jawohl*,[7]" responded Moyshe in German. "We are the Herders." And Ruchel scrunched her shoulders to help hide Saul sleeping in the shawl on her chest. Moyshe had decided to not declare the baby on the ticket.

"*Ja*[8]? *Gutt*,[9]" he answered as he marked their arrival in his ledger. "Follow everyone else."

Luckily the Wostkokoynikoff family had finished with another agent and the two families held hands, making a long chain so as not to lose anyone in the crush of people. They had little choice in where to go as the crowd moved like a herd of cattle. Almost everyone in the mass stumbled over someone else because they were too busy being awed by the ship. They had never seen a ship this close. The height of the masts, the amount of rope needed for the rigging, the water upon which the ship rested was all wonderment. An experience they never thought would be theirs.

Eventually they came to one of the two hatches that opened to the converted cargo hold below. Because of the bright daylight, they could not see what led below. A sailor was at the top calling out instructions that most of the people could not understand.

"His accent in German is terrible, but I think he says that every five people get one bunk," Moyshe explained to everyone around him.

Two sisters in poor clothing and barely fifteen asked in broken Russian, "What does this mean?"

Ruchel tried to calm them by responding, "When we get downstairs, we shall see. I'm sure everything will be fine." She wasn't sure she felt that though.

The sailor started grabbing people's bundles and tossing them below, "Down the ladder! Down the ladder!" he kept shouting. People started crying out believing their belongings were being stolen, but voices below encouraged them to come and gather their things. Down the ladder people went. It seemed to Anna they must have been standing on each other's shoulders so tightly were they sent down the ladder. Once down the ladder, people stood for a moment to adjust their eyes to the gloom.

Sheyndel started to cry, "We are going to be like animals here."

Ruchel took her disappointment out on her husband, "You paid $72 for this? And there are 5, ok 6, of us so we get one bunk? Are we animals? Are we slaves to be treated like this?"

Moyshe realized that there was to be no reasoning with her, and so instead chose to ignore most of her outrage. "So here we are, children," he said cheerily. "Let us find a bunk that will suit us before we are left with no choices."

The children had no idea of how horrific the conditions were. For them, this was still an adventure to be savored. The sawdust on the floor smelled fresh. They did not know it would not be changed during the entire voyage.

"Not too close to the hatch," called out Ruchel. "I don't want people to come by all the time and it might get cold and wet. But not too far from the hatch either. It will be far too dark."

Moyshe sighed and hoped she did not plan on nagging the entire trip. "Here," he called above the din of anxious voices. "This is the perfect one." And he picked Hannah up and sat her on the bunk.

"But Papa," whined Hannah, "I want the upstairs one."

"No, sweet child, that will be too hard to get up to and down from. This one is just fine," and he stuffed his bundle under the wide bunk for safe keeping.

Ruchel came up behind holding tightly to Saul at her breast, her bundle, and Gittel's small hand. "Anna, where is your bundle?" she asked, now busy with organizing her family. Magically from that bundle came a feather mattress that Ruchel unrolled, removing Hannah from the bunk in the process. "Now children, I want you to stay here to be safe. No wandering off. We could end up losing you." Then she took off their shoes and placed each child on the bunk with baby Saul wrapped in her shawl. She hung the boots from nails sticking out from the bunk above.

Gittel laughed, "You are decorating our bed with shoe-bells." The whole family had a laugh at that image.

Moyshe wandered off to see what their accommodations were like and Ruchel worked to arrange their bundles securely. When he returned from his wandering, he stated hopefully, "There are buckets around the space for chamber pots. This was definitely not originally designed for people, probably a cargo hold," he added more for himself.

"Moyshe, stop, the children don't need to feel like cattle or crates," his wife hissed in his ear, and she bustled around their bunk.

"Yes, dear," he whispered.

The crowd whirled around them. The children jumped every time the side of the ship was knocked as the sound vibrated throughout the hull. The buzz of numerous languages tickled their ears and the array of traditional village costumes from across Eastern Europe glowed even in the half-light of the hold. Eventually, they dropped off to sleep. While they slept, the *Bohemia* left port and started steaming up the Elbe towards the North Sea.

When the children awoke and rubbed their eyes, the hold was quieter. Not quiet, nor would it ever be during the trip. People spoke, snored, sang, coughed, and moved around. However, the anxious crying was pretty much done, plus, not everyone was in the steerage section, many were on the "tween deck" getting fresh air and watching the scenery. This was an emotional time as no one believed they would see the "Old World" ever again. They wept as the ship traveled along the river, desperately absorbing every minute of the landscape. None of this was important to the three young children. They were hungry.

"Mamma? Mamma!" cried Gittel. "I'm hungry."

Ruchel hurried over. She had found some other families from Odessa, and they had gathered to share what they knew about the upcoming trip. "Come, my chick, there is a dining hall and I hear the evening meal will be served soon," and she swiftly untied the three pairs of shoes from overhead. The children dutifully pulled them on and tied them, except for Gittel, who as the youngest had not mastered that skill. After Ruchel had inspected the three and made sure their hair was brushed and clothes were straightened, she checked the diaper on Saul. "How will I ever get these diapers clean," she mumbled as she changed him. "Children," she called out with her back to them, "do not wander far. This place is a small city and there are many dangers." They looked at each other in wonderment as to how she could know what they were doing.

Finally, baby Saul was clean and quiet, and Ruchel believed her brood would not embarrass her in their presentation. Then she sent them up the ladder and along the deck to the dining hall. It wasn't too hard to find as they could smell the food and a crowd was headed in the same direction. Just inside the entrance to the dining hall, each person was handed a tray that had a round indent intended for a cup. Then each person shuffled behind the person in front until they reached a long table with enormous bowls on it and sailors standing behind. One placed a biscuit on each tray as the person shuffled past;

the next slapped a pat of butter down; the third gave each person a cup of tea. Then people wandered off to find a place to sit. Ruchel kept her children in front of her so that she could watch them. They finally found some space at one of the long tables set up for eating. The children carefully placed their trays on the table and then the younger two clambered on their chairs and sat on their knees to reach the table. Anna, however, did her best to act like an adult. After all, she was helping take care of the little ones, as she called them in her head.

All around them people were in various states of their meals. Some were wiping their sleeves across their faces to clean their lips after finishing the meal. Other families sat in silence waiting to bless their food. Without ceremony, the Herder family began by rubbing their biscuits against the butter.

"Mamma," asked Hannah, "is this all? I thought I smelled chicken."

"I guess that is for the first-class people, not us steerage folks," sighed Ruchel. "But this is good, so eat up."

When they had all finished, Ruchel stood up and saw that people were stacking their trays on a cart by the exit door. So, she gathered their four and stacked the cups on them and then herded her offspring out onto the deck. It was a really lovely June evening, so they found a comfortable spot and watched the sun set over the banks of the Elbe slowly obscuring the towns that they had never visited and never would.

When they finally returned to their bunk, they found Moyshe rifling through one of the bundles. "Isn't there any food?" he queried.

Ruchel looked at him angrily. "Yes, and stop making such a racket and mess," she retorted as she pushed everything to one side so that she could put the baby down. "There was a meal in the dining hall. Did you miss it?" And she repacked the bundle quickly and neatly, so that the other children could climb up. "Where have you been?" she asked bit too casually as she untied shoes and hung them back up. She efficiently tucked each child in before she made herself ready for bed.

"I found some other men of thought and we were discussing what exactly the Golden Land meant to us and how we could make it a better place."

"Ah," she commented as she laid her shawl over the children and wrapped the sleeping baby in her *babushka*. "Great thoughts about a place none of you have even seen. I hope that filled your belly." Then she lay down next to Anna and tried to sleep. Her frustration at minding their four children and keeping their space organized, plus her fears made her angry at her husband who saw none of this.

Moyshe sat on the other side other bunk, a bit confused. He had had a lovely philosophical debate with a number of Russian and German men. They had debated the merits of religion in a land where there was no state religion, among other lofty ideas. He tried to convince them to join his *Am Olam* movement. What Jew wouldn't want to be part of "The Eternal People"? After all, aren't all Jews part of *Am Olam*? He had chosen the name with such a purpose. It was unfathomable to him why the men he had debated with insisted that Jews do not farm. He had quoted the Bible and they the Talmud and others just scoffed. Then he too took off his boots and hung them up, and took off his coat and covered himself and fell asleep.

5

The Crossing

The next day and all that followed for the next two weeks were pretty much the same. Everyone would rise in the morning. Some mornings were glorious and the North Sea and then the Atlantic Ocean offered a smooth sea. The families would traipse to the dining hall where they were served coffee, bread or a biscuit with butter, or even oatmeal with molasses. If the weather held, they would crowd the tween deck to get out of the stench of steerage. Some would even bring up their mattresses to air out.

On the days when the sea was rough, steerage remained crowded with people. The cacophony of the sick vomiting and groaning and the children playing made the space almost unbearable. Eventually arguments would explode between those who had bunks near the hatches and wanted them closed to keep the wet out and those further from the hatches who were desperate for fresh air and light.

The Steerage Experience
Horrors of the emigrant ship--scene in the hold of the "James Foster, Jun." United States, 1869. Library of Congress, www.loc.gov/item/92522099/.

The day was broken by an afternoon meal that filled the bellies of those who went. More people attended the meals as the voyage continued. Those who were concerned that the kitchen on board was not *kosher*[10] ate only what they had brought. Fairly quickly they realized this was not enough to make it for two weeks or more. The length of the trip could only be estimated as bad weather could make the trip longer. One by one, the religious Jewish families started to appear in the dining hall.

The midday meal was a veritable feast with soup, some kind of meat or fish, and potatoes. For most in steerage that meat was served every day was unbelievable. For those who kept *kosher*, it was problematic. Most of these people came to the conclusion that the children could eat the meat, but the adults stuck to the soup and potatoes. However, when pork was served a cry could be heard among the Jewish children as the meat was removed from their trays by their parents. That was one barrier the stringent parents could not cross.

Anna, Hannah, and Gittel would sit mesmerized by the religious Jews praying after their meals. "Why do they do that?" one would invariably ask.

Ruchel would respond with growing impatience, "They are thanking God for their meal."

"Yes, but why make such a show of it?" another would ask.

Ruchel was tired and stressed beyond limit. Moyshe spent most of his time on deck, when the weather was good, or in a quiet spot, when it was not, discussing philosophy, Zionism, farming, even theology with other men. He had little to do with the family. Ruchel was left trying to keep her brood active and in her view. She was constantly afraid that one would fall overboard or be stolen. Plus, sickness was rampant in steerage and there was no water with which to wash. Answering theological questions was never her forte and the fear of the unknown made these kinds of discussions even with a child near impossible. Her response to that question was always the same, "Ask Papa."

There were many things besides religion to fascinate the children. They could sit for hours and admire the vastness of the ocean. Everyone could. The only people on board unfazed by this phenomenon were the sailors. They were constantly rushing past carrying ropes, baskets or barrels full of materials, brooms, and items no one could identify. The boys, especially, were fond of following the sailors around and Hirsch learned to tie knots from them. Then he would come back from his adventures with bits of rope and try to teach the Herder girls to make them. Ruchel did not approve of Sheindel's free hand with her boys, especially eight-year-old Hirsch who could basically roam free. She was particularly upset when Hirsch started teaching Hannah new words in foreign languages. She was pretty sure they weren't appropriate for children, if anyone, and gave both children a stern talking to.

Anna was thrilled to get glimpses of the ladies in first class in their fine dresses. Someday, she hoped, she, Hannah, and Gittel, and Mamma, of course, would stand straight and tall in their corsets. There would be rows of flounces on their skirts over their bustles. Her mamma wore old fashioned petticoats under her dress and there no ruffles or lace. When Anna saw the fine fur muffs the ladies would take out to warm their hands at night, she would tuck her tiny hands under her shawl. No one should know they were dirty with broken nails. While the hats were to be admired, with their feathers, Anna did see the virtue in her mother's *babushka*. It kept her hair neat and ears warm.

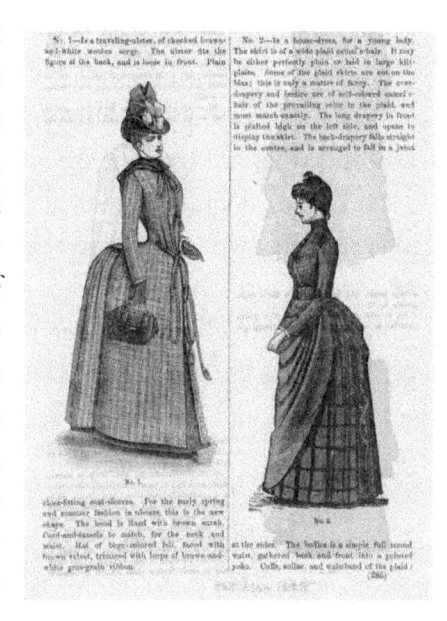

Ladies in Traveling Clothes
The New York Public Library. "Traveling ulster; House-dress for young lady, United States, 1880s" New York Public Library Digital Collections, *digitalcollections.nypl.org/items/ 510d47e0-e3ad-a3d9-e040-e00a18064a99.*

Gittel, however, was fascinated by the nuns on board. There was a small group traveling together that shared a bunk in steerage. They almost always did things in a group, like a flock of birds, thought the girl. They rose together, walked together, prayed together, ate together. Gittel wasn't sure what praying was since her family didn't, but that's what the other children told her. What awed her the most were the amazing white bonnets they wore. They were not like anything she had seen before. As wide as the wearer's shoulders, they stood out with a drape behind. Gittel was too afraid to ask them if they ironed them and folded them every day, like Mamma did her *babushka*, or if they came stitched that way. And they had big white collars almost like shawls. "How did they stay so white?" she wondered to herself.

Then one day, what Ruchel most feared happened. She was chatting with some of the other Russian women and thought Anna had Gittel with her and the other girls. When Ruchel checked, Gittel was gone. "My chick! My daughter! Anna," She screamed, "where is your sister?

Anna looked around in horror. "Gittel was just here," she responded fearfully. "At least, I thought she was," Anna whispered.

Word spread quickly that a child was missing. Mothers quickly gathered their own children to reassure themselves theirs had not been lost. Moyshe and Mordechai went searching for the little girl.

Mordechai finally found her next to a coil of rope as tall as she was. Gittel was crying. When Mordechai put his hand on her shoulder, she looked up and wiped her face on her sleeve. "I lost my mamma," she sobbed.

"Come, little one," he said reassuringly as he lifted her up in his arms. "I know where she is. She's lost you and is worried." He carried her back to Ruchel in triumph.

Upon seeing Mordechai with Gittel in his arms, Ruchel burst into tears. She handed Saul to Sheyndel and buried her daughter in her arms in a hug. "Where did you wander to?" asked Ruchel sobbing.

Nuns
Armand Gauthier, "Nuns," before 1895.

"Well, Mamma," began Gittel also sobbing, "I saw the nuns."

"The nuns, always the nuns," mumbled her mother.

"The wind came, and I had to see if they would fly away like the seagulls."

Moyshe came running up at that moment, having heard of the rescue, and embraced Ruchel and Gittel in one large hug.

"She, she,...was following the nuns," sobbed Ruchel, slowly calming down.

"Now, child," smiled Moyshe gently, "have I not told you that religion will get you in trouble. Stay near your mamma. I intend to keep all my children."

6

The Embarkation

On June 21 a cry went up among the steerage passengers, "We are there!" And then a chant of "America" was heard. Everyone left the steerage hold for the tween deck. It was true – there was the American coastline. What the immigrants did not know was there was still a while to travel. They were only seeing the eastern end of Long Island. The ship had to follow the coast and sail up the Lower and Upper Bays to get to Castle Garden at the southern tip of Manhattan where they could all then disembark. They all pushed to the starboard side of the ship. Everyone wanted to see the Golden Land, their new home.

Suddenly, over the bull horn the captain's voice was commanding: "Everyone cannot rush to one side. Please, some of you must move to the port side before we tip over!"

Castle Gardens with the Statue of Liberty, between 1880 and 1897
William Henry Jackson, "New York Bay, Castle Gardens," Detroit Publishing Co. New York Bay, Library of Congress, www.loc.gov/item/2016817501/.

Everyone stopped and looked at each other. Then other voices broadcast the same announcement over the bull horn in a variety of languages. A wail arose and people dutifully ran to the other side of the ship to make sure they did not tip into the water. For the rest of the day, people took turns watching the New World pass by.

In the morning, an immigration official came on board to review the manifest with the captain and examine the sick. Nothing that could start an epidemic would be allowed off the ship. He traveled with the *Bohemia* up the bays and made sure no one on board communicated with anyone on land. Very quickly the official became unimportant as the immigrants marveled at the sights along the Bay: churches, factories, and more. Not one of the passengers could have imagined such wonders in their hometowns. Even those from European cities were in awe. They were sure that because this was America, everything thing was different. When they left the Upper Bay and anchored in the stream just away from Castle Garden, the immigration officer left the ship and was replaced by a member of the Metropolitan Police force.

The passengers were getting anxious. They were so close to their destination they could wave at the people on shore, but they could not get off the ship. Rumors started to spread: They were being sent back, someone on board had the plague, there was a murderer in their midst. People began to cry. A few kind sailors tried to calm the crowd, explaining in broken German that "this is the way. Everything to be checked. No worries."

Eventually, landing agents boarded the ship and began to inspect the luggage. Since they, of course, began with the first-class passengers, the steerage passengers began the rumors again. This time, it was that not everyone would be allowed to disembark because of a limit on immigrants. This fear grew worse when the steerage passengers saw the first-class luggage being lowered onto the barges to be moved to the dock. Then the first-class passengers were assisted into the tugboats that had come abreast of the big ship.

Finally, the agents got to the steerage passengers. The sailors had forced everyone back into the hold and only allowed one family or passenger up at a time to keep the agents from being crushed by the crowd. The agents had the passengers open their bundles, retie them, and then head to the tugs.

Ruchel had been listening to the gossip and become fearful. "What if they run out of space in America before we are checked?" she asked Moyshe.

"Come now," he said, "you read the letters from our comrades here as well as I did. They said to be patient and we shall all get off the ship."

So, the family waited as patiently as they could on the bunk. Moyshe and Ruchel had the knowledge that their name would be called, and they would leave the ship for New York. Moyshe wandered at times and tried to calm his nervous fellow passengers. He attempted to reassure them that everyone would have a chance above.

Eventually, their name was called. Once again everyone took their bundles and made their way towards the ladder. Ruchel went up first with Saul strapped to her. Then the children followed, climbing the ladder with expertise. Finally, Moyshe handed up the bundles and followed. As they stood before the agent who untied their bundles and poked around their few possessions, Ruchel again got nervous.

"Where are Mordechai and his family?" she whispered to her husband.

"Hush," he responded. As the family made their way to their tugboat he reassured his wife, "We both have the address of our lodgings in New York City. If nothing else, we will meet there."

At the pier, Hannah pointed out a small steam ship docked there, "Look, Papa! Another steamship. I wonder where we go on that."

"We are not going on that. God forbid," he responded. "I've been told that ship takes the very ill to a hospital." The family passed safely through the health inspection at the pier and moved to the Rotunda.

Arriving at Castle Gardens
"Immigrants landing at Castle Garden", The Miriam and Ira D. Wallach Division of Art, Prints and Photographs: Picture Collection, New York Public Library Digital Collections, digitalcollections.nypl.org/items/ 510d47e1-0f5b-a3d9-e040-e00a18064a99.

"This place frightens me," whispered Ruchel to her husband as they followed the crowd. "It looks more like a fortress than a port. Maybe they will keep us here and not let us pass."

"Foolish woman," he whispered to himself in frustration.

In the Rotunda, the family was registered. Moyshe answered questions in German about who they were and where they were going. He was very proud to say that he already had a place for his family to live and promises of a job. They were directed to the Exchange Brokers who took what rubles they had and gave them dollars instead. The family gathered round their new currency, on display in Moyshe's hand.

"Who is that?" asked Anna pointing to George Washington on the $1 bills her father held. "Is that the czar of America?"

Ruchel laughed, "There is no czar here, child. That is one of the reasons we came. But I don't know who that is."

"He must be important," Hannah said.

Moyshe studied him closer, "I would like his head of hair." He took off his hat and ran his fingers through his thinning hair. The girls giggled and their father put his hat back on.

Dollar Bill

The family held tight to each other as they made their way to the Castle Garden exit. As if by magic, Mordechai, Sheyndel, and their boys were waiting for them at the exit. The crush of people made it nearly impossible for the Herders to stop, so Moyshe waved at them to follow.

7

The Reunion

They found a place to stop and rest at a park not far from Castle Garden. There Mordechai and his family found them. Everyone was hungry, but their supply of food had disappeared very quickly on the ship.

"Look!" shouted Hirsch pointing further into the park, "A man with a basket of nuts." The children all started waving at him to come closer.

Seeing the children dancing and waving at him, the nut vender came over. This was why he was in the park. He knew many of the immigrants walked through the park on the way to the Lower East Side and he knew he could make an excellent profit on them. As he approached, he removed his hat and made a small bow to the ladies.

Mordechai approached him. After two weeks on the ship with people from all over Europe, he had become rather adept at sign language. "How much for a cone of nuts?" he inquired pointing to the wares and then making a cone out of his hands.

The vender held up a cone and tilted his head. Mordechai nodded yes in response.

"One penny," replied the vender holding up his index finger.

Mordechai thought for a moment and held up nine fingers. Everyone was starving; this was their first meal in their new country. The vender nodded yes as well. Mordechai pulled out his change purse and realized he had no idea what the coins were in his purse. He selected one silver one; it was larger than the rest. The vender took it and gave Mordechai three coins in return: two silver ones of different sizes and a copper one. Then he gently handed each child a paper cone of nuts, graciously bowed to the women when he handed them theirs, and finally gave Moyshe and Mordechai theirs. Having completed the transaction, he went to the next group of hungry and weary travelers humming in the sunshine.

Everyone greedily opened their cones to start their feast and then stopped short.

"What is this?" Sheyndel asked holding up a peanut.

Ruchel started to giggle, "It looks deformed."

"No," Anna said. "It's twins. All of them are twins."

Gittel dumped hers into her skirt spread across her lap to see if this were true.

"Well," Mordechai began slowly. "They are nuts, so we eat them. And they are nuts, so we have to get the meat out of the shells."

"But," interjected his wife, "we've no nut cracker." Little Mendel started to cry.

Moyshe clenched his fist in frustration around the peanuts he had in his hand. He paused and stared at his hand as he opened it. The shells were cracked and crumbling. "Well, this should be fairly easy," he announced. "Look, the shells are soft." Everyone gathered round his hand, which he held low enough for the children to see. A round of "ahs" went through the group.

Then everyone settled down in the grass under a tree to eat the new treat. The children gleefully tossed the soft-shell bits around them. Having been cooped up shipboard and being very careful to not make a tense situation worse, they enjoyed the freedom to be messy and loud.

After eating a few of the small nut meats, Ruchel turned to Moyshe, "What do you think of this New World food?"

He paused for a moment and cocked his head to think. "I have certainly never tasted anything like it. Definitely different than a chestnut or walnut. Maybe akin to a hazel nut in size and texture, but without a doubt this is different."

Sheyndel noted, "The children seem to be enjoying not only the nuts, but the friendly squirrels." And the three other adults turned to see the children tossing shells and a few nuts at the squirrels who had gathered near them. The four parents laughed in the sunshine with joy and relief.

When everyone had finished, they stood up and brushed the peanut shells and dust off their clothes. As they collected the bundles and the children, they looked around. Odessa was nothing compared to New York City, and they had only seen a small part.

Moyshe pointed at the broad road and announced, "We will follow this wide road. Certainly, people will help us along the way." Since they had really only one direction to travel, everyone agreed. Once they reached the avenue, they stopped in awe.

In a hushed tone, Hannah said, "It goes on forever. Look, there is no end."

"Look how wide it is," Hirsch added. "An army could march down this street."

"Indeed," his father responded. "And it is time for our army to march this road." He took his son's hand and started marching north up Broadway Avenue. The two looked quite comical marching like soldiers, but they were happy in their mutual adventure.

It wasn't that they had never seen three or four storied buildings; rather, it was the vast number of these buildings with flags on their roofs that amazed this small group of Russian immigrants. They took their time gawking at the buildings, the trolley tracks, and the fine clothes most of the people wore walking the street. There were also a great number of horses pulling wagons.

Eventually they came across the most amazing church they had ever seen. It was not like the ones they were used to with onion shapes on the towers. This one looked like it was covered in lace made from stone. It filled an entire block. People wandered in and out of one of the three tall double doors. None of the Herders or Wostokoynikoffs had ever entered a church, and none planned to, but they could not help but gaze at the religious monument that was St. Paul's Cathedral.

St. Paul's Cathedral
"St. Paul's Cathedral, New York," The Miriam and Ira D. Wallach Division of Art, Prints and Photographs: Photography Collection, New York Public Library Digital Collections, nypl.getarchive.net/media/st-pauls-cathedral-new-york-eb328b.

Another long walk, or so it seemed to little Mendel, and they came upon another stone building.

"Just like a wedding cake," was Gittel's humbled statement.

"So it is," her mother responded mouth agape.

Hirsh stopped still and announced, "It isn't a box. Aren't buildings supposed to be boxes?"

Sheyndel remarked, "Look at all those columns, on every floor. And windows in the roof."

"It must be an important building," commented Moyshe. "Look! Everyone goes in that comes by. Someday we too will stop here and go inside, but today we have to find our new home."

Post Office
"Post office, New York City," The Miriam and Ira D. Wallach Division of Art, Prints and Photographs: Photography Collection, New York Public Library Digital Collections, digitalcollections.nypl.org/items/ 510d47e1-ea7e-a3d9-e040-e00a18064a99.

They walked a little way on and Moyshe signaled for them to halt. He walked up to a coachman. "Excuse me, sir," he said removing his hat. "I heard you speak to your horse in Russian. How pleasant it is to hear a familiar language in this strange land."

The man in his fine uniform looked at the obvious immigrant with suspicion and immediately arranged it so his horse was between the two men. Speaking over the horse's muzzle, he asked, "What do you want?"

"Goodness," Moyshe replied, "There is no need to be curt. My family, friends, and I are a bit lost and need some help finding an address." He put his bundle down and started searching his pockets. "Ah, here it is," he said to himself totally unaware the coachman was becoming more and more uncomfortable. "I'm afraid I cannot even read this as I haven't learned English yet," so he handed the scrap of paper over the horse's muzzle to the man opposite.

The coachman barely touched the paper before returning it. "So, there is a park behind me with two large buildings."

"Yes," Moyshe nodded, "we saw the one that looked like a wedding cake."

"Fine, that's the post office and the other is the city hall. Cut between them and turn left to follow in the same direction you were going. When you come to the end of the next park turn right and eventually you will get there." And then he dismissed Moyshe by adjusting the horse's straps.

Moyshe returned his hat to his head, put the paper back in his pocket, collected his bundle, opened his mouth to say thanks and closed it again because the coachman had walked away. Thus, Moyshe returned to his waiting family and friends. "At least we have some idea of where to go now," he remarked.

"How much further must we walk?" an exhausted Hannah asked.

"That I do not know, my poor child, but we walk through this amazing park," and thus he led the group. Through City Hall Park they wandered, agog at what they now knew to be the amazing post office and the equally impressive city hall. The children all insisted they stop and stare at the fountain and refused to go further until they had washed their hands and faces in the sparkling water. Only then would they trudge onward.

City Hall Park
"The park and City Hall, New York," The Miriam and Ira D. Wallach Division of Art, Prints and Photographs: Print Collection, New York Public Library Digital Collections, https://digitalcollections.nypl.org/items/ 510d47da-f984-a3d9-e040-e00a18064a99

They did not know the names of the streets they walked, Centre and then Worth, but it became apparent to even little Mendel that the city was changing. The roads changed not only because they were getting narrower, but the buildings were less grand and eventually became quite plain. The people became more worn and their clothes more practical, like what the two families were wearing. The streets grew crowded with pushcarts and the chaos of children running in the street.

At one point, the families stopped and stared at the strange people with straight black hair, jaundiced skin, and slanted eyes.

Anna pointed and laughed, "Mamma, look at that man! His braid is longer than mine."

Her mother slapped down her hand, "Don't point. You don't want people to know how ignorant you are."

Moyshe came up behind them, "I've seen a few men like that at the port in Odessa. Those are Chinamen. They are people just like us. They talk with another language and their clothes are different, but that makes no matter." And he took Anna's hand and dragged her forward.

Now Moyshe and Mordechai kept their papers with the apartment address in their hands and every time they passed someone who spoke Russian they asked for directions. Finally, they arrived at a grey tenement building.

"Here we are," announced Moyshe with much bravado.

Tenement
New York City - The old and the new styles of tenement houses / from sketches by a staff artist. New York, 1882. Library of Congress, www.loc.gov/item/96506802/.

"This?" Ruchel affirmed quizzically and then sighed. New York was only going to be temporary, her husband had promised, but this was a disappointment.

They walked up the outside stairs and opened the front door. The building was well used and clearly someone did their best to keep it clean.

"Hallo?" cried out Moyshe. "I hear that is how Americans greet each other," he said to his fellow travelers.

"Is that?" called a woman's voice from the second floor. "I know that voice." And a frazzled woman came dashing down the staircase wiping her hands on her apron. "Moyshe! Ruchel! Mordechai! And Sheyndel! And the children. Oh, who is this wee one?" the words tumbled out without a pause.

"Dina?" Ruchel chirped. "Oh, how I've missed you." The two friends hugged tightly.

"Come upstairs. You must be tired. I've got some soup. We've been waiting for you," Dina continued breathlessly. She grabbed Mendel's hand and Hirsch's bundle and led everyone upstairs. "We all live here. The entire Odessa *Am Olam*. Everyone will be excited when they come home from work and see you here." As she led them into one of the apartments. Here the main room was filled with the smell of potato soup and starch. Dina had been pressing the laundry. "Come sit and I will get you all some soup and bread."

The children dropped their bundles and eagerly took places around the table. Their parents moved those bundles against the walls in piles. They then took seats around the table as well. Dina took a stack of unmatched bowls and mugs from the single shelf on the wall and a handful of spoons out of a drawer. Then she carefully filled each bowl or mug with fresh hot potato soup.

"Who is this little fella?" asked Dina holding Saul.

"Oh, our Saul," began Ruchel gently, "he was born after you left. I didn't even know I was pregnant for quite a while."

"Tell us about our friends here," demanded Moyshe. "Your letters have been too filled with business and too little information."

"We live here together like a big family, just like in Odessa," began Dina. "It is of course harder because we all have not learned English, but that will come. Anushka and Dovid and Michael are taking evening classes to learn English. Then they are teaching us. Alexi and Stephan, Erik, and Yury are outside the city working on farms. They visit when they can and bring their earnings too. So far," she continued without pause, "they are enjoying the experience. Hopefully, what they learn will help us when we buy our farms."

"Oh hush," interrupted Sheyndel, "You are giving me a headache. We have been traveling for a month. We've been in crowds and trains and cargo holds. I could so do with some silence."

Mendel hung his head as though reprimanded, and the other children giggled.

"I'll save the rest of the news for later," Dina smiled. "When you have finished, I'll show where you are sleeping. I can even get out the tub and we can arrange for some baths."

Soon enough, everyone had their fill of soup, and they were feeling sleepy. Dina took them across the hall to another apartment. There two rooms had been reserved for the two families. Sheyndel and Ruchel got the children ready for bed. For the first time in a long time the children undressed in relative privacy and lay down in a quiet bed.

Then Sheyndel and Ruchel joined their husbands in the kitchen. Moyshe had unpacked the *samovar* and was busy filling it with coals and water and tea. He smiled at Ruchel as he did so.

"Now," she said. "It is home"

Once the adults had a cup of tea, they went to bed as well. Dina went back to her laundry across the hall.

8

A New Beginning

When the two families finally awoke it was early evening. Clearly people had been in the apartment, the dining table had been moved aside and a bathtub was now in the middle of the room. A stack of drying sheets was on the table. Draped over the various chairs was an array of men's coats. Across the hall there was laughter and singing. Unable to contain themselves, the children ran across the hall in their nightshirts. There they were greeted with much joy. The adults decided to dress before they reunited with their friends.

Once dressed, they joined the rest of the *Am Olam* community across the hall. Upon their entrance the entire group let out a joyous hurrah. Everyone stood up and chairs were knocked over in haste. No family reunion could have been more joyful.

"A celebration!" called out Abraham. "Bring out the vodka!!"

Magically a number of bottles of homemade vodka appeared at the table. Dina uncovered glasses, cups, and mugs of all kinds and the adults raised a toast and then another. Singing began. Eventually brown bread and cheese were passed around. Finally, everyone went to bed.

Ruchel marveled at the number of people in their apartment. Each family had a room and the other two bedrooms each had four men, two to a bed. Then another three men found space in the living room.

"Amazing how we can all live here," she remarked. "How long will we stay here?"

"Only until we save enough money to buy the farm," Moyshe replied. "The group here has already made some good headway. Now that we are here, saving should go even faster."

"I hope it is fast. I feel like a sardine crammed into a can. How so many people can live together in such little space is amazing and frightening," was the answer in the dark.

Once they were in their nightshirts, they climbed into the narrow double bed. Moyshe pulled his wife close, and they fell asleep.

Anna woke up to hear Saul crying. She rolled out of bed and picked up her baby brother. Her parents weren't around. Then she heard splashing in the kitchen. Opening the door, she stepped into the kitchen, quickly and quietly shutting the door behind her. She saw her mother sitting in the tub in the middle of the kitchen. Sheindel stood by the stove warming another kettle of water. On the edge of the tub rested a bar of soap just like the ash and fat soap they used at home and her mother was busy scrubbing her legs with a pumice stone.

"Momma," Anna whispered, "Saul was crying. He's busy suckling on my finger."

"Bring him here," laughed her mother. "No unswaddle him, might as well give him a bath."

Anna dutifully unwrapped her bother and handed him to their mother. Ruchel put Saul to her breast and gently poured water over him. When he finished suckling, Ruchel rested him on her legs and rubbed the soap all over him. Then she dunked him quickly in the tub.

"Quickly Sheyndel, come take Saul," she commanded.

Dutifully Sheyndel came over with a drying sheet. "Hush, sweet boy," she cooed as she laid him on the table and dried him carefully. Then she grabbed a diaper and expertly folded and pinned it. Finally, she took a clean blanket and wrapped him up.

While all this was going on, Ruchel climbed out of the tub and wrapped herself in a series of drying sheets. As she moved toward the sink, she motioned at Anna.

"Into the tub you go."

"Mamma?"

"Everyone gets a bath today. No arguing."

Anna knew from her mother's tone of voice there really wasn't any arguing. With resignation, she pulled her nightshirt off over her head and stepped into the tepid water. Sheyndel came with a pot and a kettle. First, she scooped out a pot of water and then she poured in the kettle of hot water. Carefully, she carried the pot of water over to the dry sink where Ruchel was already rubbing vinegar into her hair. After she had rubbed the vinegar from her scalp to the ends of her hair, she dumped the tepid tub water over her hair to rinse it.

"Anna, don't forget to use the soap," she suggested as she wrapped her hair in a sheet. Then she got dressed. As Ruchel put on each layer of clothing, Anna watched enviously how she so wanted to be a grown-up with real lady's clothing. First her mother put on her chemise and pantaloons and then her corset. On top of this went a series of petticoats and then her dress. There were a lot of buttons to be done, but finally her mother looked proper again.

Sheyndel helped Anna out of the tub and wrapped her in a sheet. Ruchel pointed to the sink. Anna sighed. She hated smelling like vinegar, but at least she only had her hair washed every few weeks.

"Wake up, sweet sleepers," called Sheyndel. "Bath time."

"No, Mamma," responded Hirsch.

"You do not get to say no to me. I am your mother. You are next. Out of bed and into the tub."

"Boys don't take baths," he retorted.

"I'm sorry. Your father and Mr. Herder have already taken theirs. Now..." and she stormed back to the kitchen.

Ruchel had finished washing Anna's hair. Anna sat on a chair with one sheet wrapped around her and the other around her head. Ruchel was brushing her own hair as Hirsch stumbled into the room. Ruchel graciously turned her back as Hirsch took off his nightshirt and stepped into the tub. As Sheyndel did not trust her son to do a good job, she took the soap and pumice and scrubbed him herself. Anna watched as

Ruchel brushed and braided her hair. By this time Hannah, Gittel, and Mendel were up and came into the kitchen.

"Go, Anna, go get dressed," commanded her mother. Anna complied. Keeping the sheet wrapped tightly around herself she dashed back to the bedroom.

"Out of the tub," Sheyndel nudged Hirsch.

"Nope, not with girls in the room."

"Hannah and Gittel will turn their backs."

Since they did, Hirsch got out of the tub and let his mother dry him and wrap him in a sheet. Then she sent him over to Ruchel to have his hair washed. Again, Scheindel took a pot of water from the tub and put a kettle of hot water in.

"Ok girls, you next" announced Ruchel and she poured water over Hirsch's head.

Hannah and Gittel loved time in the bath. They couldn't understand why they didn't get to play in the water more often. Unabashed about Hirsch and Mendel in the room, they stripped and practically jumped into the tub. Splashing about they scrubbed each other. At one point, Gittel disappeared, and Hannah held up Gittel's foot.

"Please, don't drown each other," begged Ruchel playfully as Gittel reemerged.

"My turn!" cried out Mendel, jealous of the girls' fun.

"You are right, my son," Sheyndel agreed. "We cannot spend all day cleaning ourselves. There is much more to do today." And she lifted one and then the other girl out of the tub and slipped her son in.

As Sheyndel scrubbed the last child, Ruchel dried off her girls. After placing a chair in front of the sink, she lifted Hannah up to wash her hair and, when finished, she did the same with Gittel. While the children dressed, the women emptied the tub and put it in the corner of the kitchen. They returned the table to its rightful place and tossed all the sheets in the tub.

"Breakfast," called out Ruchel and the children bounded into the room and took their places at the table. Sheyndel poured everyone a cup of tea and Ruchel put a plate with a slice of bread and hunk of cheese by each child.

"Now children," began Ruchel. "Here we all work together. So, Sheyndel and I are going to take care of everyone – we will run this home for everyone, and you all are going to help us."

"Where is Papa?" asked Mendel.

"Your papas are both out looking for work," answered Sheyndel. "The other men are helping them find work. Now, what jobs will you have?"

"And what are you going to do?" asked Hirsch.

"Well, Ruchel and I have decided that along with taking care of you and everyone we will help support our commune and save money for a farm by taking in laundry."

"And how can we help?" asked Anna.

"Well, there is much to do. First, you will all share the responsibilities of emptying the chamber pots into the outhouse."

"Oh, ewwwww," Gittel moaned.

"Someone has to do it. Then you will sweep the apartments and stairwell."

"Really?" Hannah asked.

"That's work for girls," complained Hirsch.

"Son, that is work so that we can all become the farmers we wish to. This is why we came all the way to America."

"What else can we do," offered Anna.

"We will see as we follow our days," answered Ruchel. "Now that breakfast is over, we must all begin our chores." As an example, she cleared the table and put the dishes in the sink.

The children scattered to find the chamber pots in various rooms in the building. The women each took a bucket and they all traipsed down the two flights of stairs to the tiny courtyard behind the building. There the children took turns emptying the pots into the outhouse and the women pumped water into their buckets to fill them. After making sure the children washed the pots and themselves at the pump, they all returned upstairs.

As Ruchel began washing the dishes, theirs and the ones everyone else had left earlier in the morning, Sheindel handed out the brooms.

"Where is Dina?" Hirsch asked. He had been quite charmed by the chatty young lady.

"Well," replied his mother. "Since we are here and have to stay home to care for all of you, she went to find a job as well. Every penny that can be earned gets us closer to that farm." She took the wash tub and washboard and loaded their dirty clothes into it and then tossed in a bar of lye soap. "Make sure you sweep out all the corners," She called over her shoulder as lugged the tub downstairs to the courtyard.

Upstairs the children pushed aside tables and chairs, beds, and dressers to get to every corner in the commune's various apartments. They too were going to help get everyone to the farm. Ruchel had moved all the dishes to one kitchen and stacked them on the end of one table that she'd moved near the sink. She dissolved some soap in one bucket of water and scrubbed the dishes in that. Then she put them in the sink. Once she had finished, she dumped first the bucket of dirty water and then the clean over the dishes. Finally, she took what served as a towel and began to dry them. Eventually, all the dishes were clean and stacked on the table. By now the children had returned from sweeping.

"Now, your job is to put all these dishes away, without breaking them. I am going downstairs to help Scheindel with the laundry," announced Ruchel. She put Saul in a box she had found and had lined with blankets and carried him downstairs.

Sheyndel had a pile of dirty clothes next to her on the ground. Sweat was running down her face and her sleeves were rolled up, as she bent over the washboard. Ruchel noticed a number of shirts and camisoles hanging on the line.

"The children found another basin and washboard. Should I bring it down and help with all of this?" asked Ruchel.

"Would any woman reject help with all this laundry?" chuckled Sheyndel. "Leave the baby here."

And back up the two flights went Ruchel to bring down the other wash tub and board. Since the children had finished their chores,

Ruchel told them they could play in the apartment. After tossing any other dirty clothes she found around into the tub, she lugged it all downstairs. With Sheyndel, she scrubbed and laughed and gossiped until the children came downstairs.

"Mamma," cried Mendel, "We are hungry. Can we have some lunch?"

Sheyndel brushed her arm against her forehead to wipe off the sweat. "Oh goodness," she commented as she looked up. "It is late. Look at the sun. I will come up and fix some lunch. Ruchel are you almost finished?"

"Oh, yes, go ahead. I'll finish and come follow."

"Stand back, children!" Sheyndel commanded and then turned the tub over, flooding the courtyard with soapy water.

Hirsch gave a wild yelp. Then his mother turned over the up-ended tub, put the washboard back in it and started upstairs. The children followed behind like ducklings.

After Ruchel hung up the last shirt on the laundry line, she too up ended her tub and watched the river of soapy water float away. Then she grabbed her tub and washboard and went upstairs. There she found the children contently munching on bread and cheese and gulping down water. Ruchel sat down as well. Anna passed her a plate that held a thick slice of bread and a piece of cheese. Scheindel came over with a mug and the jug of water.

When everyone had finished eating, the women sent the children into the courtyard to play. Ruchel and Sheindel stacked the dirty dishes.

"What shall we do to add to the saving? Do you really want to do laundry?" asked Sheindel.

"Oh heavens, I don't think I could spend all my time doing laundry," her friend laughed.

"How about we take in some piece work?"

"That's probably a good idea. We can get at least the two older girls to help."

"We will talk with the others when they get home. They should have some ideas on how to arrange that. Now, we have an army of people to prepare dinner for." And the two women dug through the supplies to see what they could concoct.

When the rest of the commune arrived later in the evening, pots of soup simmered on the stove and fresh bread had come out of the oven. The children, having already eaten, sat on the floor and played. Some adults sat at the table slurping their soup and munching their bread. They spoke over each other, all trying to tell each other of their days. Finally, there was a pause.

"We found work," Moyshe stated now that he had finished eating. "It is not glamorous by any means, but it is honest. Mordechai and I have factory jobs."

"The hours are long," interrupted Mordechai sadly.

"Yes, but it is not forever," interjected Moyshe positively.

"And Dina?" asked Sheindel.

"Oh yes," she replied. "I have gotten a job in a garment factory. Have you all settled in?"

"We have figured out how to run this home and to make some money," answered Ruchel. "We decided to take in piece work. How do we arrange it?"

"Oh, the factory I work in offers those jobs," offered Marta. "I could collect your work and take it back."

"That would save time," interjected Mark.

"And the children?" asked Stephan. At that the children stopped chatting and listened in.

"Well, the girls can certainly help with the sewing," commented Ruchel.

"And Mendel is far too young to work," added Scheindel. "But Hirsh is a problem."

"What have I done wrong?" queried Hirsch.

"Oh," laughed Mordechai, "it is not that you've done anything wrong, rather you are between ages."

"What about school?" Marta asked.

"School is not in session in the summer," Moyshe answered. "And we don't plan on staying long enough to make that worthwhile."

"What about a paperboy?" Dina suggested.

"I don't want him too far until he learns English," Sheyndel interjected.

"He could come to the factory and work," suggested Mark.

Mordechai shouted, "No! I am in the factory and I dislike it. Why force that on a child for even a short time?"

"That only leaves him helping us with the piece work," sighed Sheyndel.

"Girl's work?" Hirsch groaned.

Moyshe laughed, "Plenty of men are tailors and they had to start somewhere. It's a good skill to have."

"And then I can keep an eye on you," added his mother.

In this way, the two families settled into the routine of the commune. Sheyndel and Ruchel looked after everyone, doing the cooking, cleaning, and laundry. Every morning, the members rose from their beds in the various rooms in the building. They washed their faces, did their hair, and dressed. Ruchel and Sheyndel made sure coffee and oatmeal were ready for everyone. After they had left for their factory jobs, the children washed the dishes. If there was laundry to do, Ruchel took the washtub and board and the clothes to the courtyard. Despite the fifty members of the commune, because of their limited wardrobe laundry day was rarely more than once a week. No matter laundry or not, Sheyndel got started on the piece work. Sometimes, she was adding lace to lady's collars that the factory workers added to the dresses. Sometimes they made silk flowers for hats. On occasion, they put buttons on cuffs and shirt fronts. When Ruchel and the children finished their other chores, they joined Sheyndel at the table. While stitching, Sheyndel and Ruchel would have the children repeat addition and multiplication tables. They taught the children Ukrainian and Jewish folk songs and history. The members handed over their pay to Moyshe who gave a portion to the two women to buy food and cleaning supplies. Moyshe saved the rest to buy farmland and supplies.

The summer passed to fall. Now the older children were sent to school and helped when they got home and on the weekends. Ruchel and Sheyndel did not remark that Moyshe had promised they'd be gone before school began. The realization of how little everyone got paid had proven strong. However, there was no disagreement the children should go to school. Education would ensure their future. Even the children, at first, found school better than staying home to work.

Because of the long workdays and seven-day work week, no member of *Am Olam* had time to admire the glory of the fall leaves. There were few trees in the Lower East Side of Manhattan and the factories required their workers in before dawn and did not release them until well after dark. Moyshe made sure to buy a copy of *Das New Yorker Volkszeitung*[11] every day. He read this socialist newspaper to those interested after dinner. There were no Russian language papers, and the adults could not yet read English. It was from that German language paper that they learned about American politics and the growing labor movement. There were even articles about American culture to help the immigrants become Americanized.

"Listen to this," announced Moyshe one night. "There is an American holiday that celebrates how thankful Americans are for being in this great land."

Sheyndel, who loved America despite the hard work, demanded more information, "how does one celebrate this wonderful event?"

"Hmmmmmm....," Moyshe pondered as he read. "It says there is a meal like the one shared by the first settlers and savage Indians."

"Savages?" Ruchel repeated.

"What is the meal?" Sheyndel asked.

"Turkey, roast potatoes, green beans, cranberry sauce, and pumpkin and apple pies," he answered. Then he continued to read the paper.

"When is this great day?" Sheyndel continued.

"Let's see. The last Thursday of the month."

"Oh," she considered, "That's next week." She wandered off to start washing the dinner dishes.

"Oh no!" Moyshe called out.

Ruchel put down her sewing and other commune members gathered round. "What is it?" they asked.

"There was another pogrom. This time not only were businesses and homes destroyed, but there were deaths."

A hush fell over everyone.

Dina remarked, "We are lucky to be here where we are safe."

Ruchel added, "We should be thankful."

"Indeed," answered her husband.

The next morning Sheyndel announced to Ruchel, "We should have a Thanksgiving."

"But do we have the money for the special foods?" Ruchel inquired.

"We have potatoes," laughed her friend. "I'm sure we can get a chicken or two. I think we can make some kind of apple pie. We have much to be thankful for."

"Indeed," Ruchel replied. "We are safe and have a future. Who would have thought Jews could own land, and soon we will."

The following week on Thursday, the last Thursday of November 1882, Sheyndel and Ruchel planted two large pots on the dining table.

"What's this?" asked Mark.

"It is Thanksgiving, and we have chicken and potato soup to celebrate," announced Sheyndel with pride.

"And we all thank you," chimed in Dina.

The exhausted members of the commune passed their bowls dutifully to Ruchel and Sheyndel. The long days were taking their toll on them. When the pots were empty, Scheindel removed them and put a pile of fried apple wedges in its place.

"On special days, we should do something special. Happy Thanksgiving!" announced Sheyndel. She was a bit disappointed that everyone was not as excited as she was, but she was well aware how tired they were.

The days went on. On occasion Moyshe and Ruchel dipped into the savings to buy some shirting. At nine cents a yard, this was dear, but one could not stop children from growing. Mendel and Saul's clothes could be made from the older children's, but Hirsh's and Anna's had to come from somewhere.

Winter came just as fall had come. Everyone was glad they had brought their coats and boots with them. The children came home singing songs that their parents didn't understand. When asked, they called them Christmas carols.

Late one night Ruchel woke her husband, "Do we care about these Christmas carols?"

Moyshe was exhausted; he had no time for chatter, "It is America. This is what they do, so this is what we do."

Ruchel continued to worry, "But what if our children become Christians?"

Moyshe turned to face his wife in the dark of the room, "Ruchel, we won't be here long enough for that to happen. Let me sleep." And he turned his back on his wife and immediately began to snore.

And then everything changed. Hirsch came running upstairs one afternoon. "Mamma! Mamma!" he shouted. "A letter!"

"Come now, child," she reprimanded. "It isn't like we don't get letters."

"Well, yes, letters from Ukraine, but this one is from America," retorted Hirsh.

"What? Who would write us in this country?" Sheyndel asked as she studied the envelope. She could not read English, so she did not know where the letter was from or who sent it, but the stamps were ones she did not recognize. They were slate blue and had an oval on them with a bust of a man she did not recognize. Clearly, he was important because he was on the stamp. "But," she thought, "how unbecoming he is with a bald head and a double chin." She could not read what was written on the stamps other than the numeral "1." With a deadline looming on her piece work and there being no one around to explain what was written on the envelope, Sheyndel put it the envelope with the two slate blue stamps that carried images of Benjamin Franklin on the shelf where their can of household money was kept. When the rest of the commune came home, she would give it to Moyshe.

Postage Stamp

In dashed Anna with Hannah and Gittel in tow. "Where is it? Where is the American letter?" she demanded.

Knowing there was no way these children would return to their chores if she didn't show them the letter, she put down the sewing she was working on and stood up. "No opening or messing this envelope," she reprimanded them and then returned to her work.

The girls passed the envelope among them, studying the writing, even though they could read printed letters in a book, handwriting was still beyond their skill. Then they dropped the envelope on the table and went back to washing the dishes across the hall. When Sheyndel took a break, she put it back on the shelf.

After a simple supper that evening of bread and cheese many of the members wandered off to bed. It was then that Sheyndel remembered the letter and took it off the shelf and handed it to Moyshe.

"I do not know who this is for, but as leader of our group, I figured you should have it," offered Sheyndel.

"Well, let us take a look," stated Moyshe and he took the letter. He could not read the envelope either, but that did not stop him from slicing it open with a knife. Then he gently pulled the letter out, and majestically unfolded the paper sheets inside and sat back to read it. "It is in Russian from our friends all the way west in the state called Arkansas."

"Ar-kan-sas, I wonder where that is?" pondered Hirsch.

"Read on," demanded Dina.

"Ahem," declared Moyshe as much to clear his throat as to gain everyone's attention. The room was quite full as word had spread throughout the building that a letter had come. People had flung open their bedroom doors and it was standing room only in the apartment and the hallway. The children had been passed over everyone and now sat on the table with Saul resting in Anna's lap.

From in the hallway someone shouted, "Moyshe, stand up, shout it out so we can all hear!"

In compliance, Moyshe stood up and began in a large voice:

"20 March 1883

Dear Friends,

We have arrived safely, all of us. The trip was certainly not as arduous as from the Old Country. It was all by train. New York City to St. Louis was quite civilized and safe, though clearly as we went west it became more rugged. In St. Louis, we changed to a more local train that took us to the town of Newport. We figured out there must be around 700 in the town. Word spread that we had arrived, and some men came over to speak with us. Those among us who knew English spoke with these men, who we discovered were merchants and Jewish. The most important Jew in Newport is Simon Adler who has helped many, from what he said, get started.

He explained he was willing to help us. When we explained that we had come well prepared, Adler simply said he was willing to help in any way and pointed us on our way.

And so we gathered all 150 of us and collected our baggage that had been left at the depot and began our walk to our land. It took two days as we had almost 15 miles to go, but we did not care.

We have found Eden! It is spring and the trees are just starting to open. The woods are thick and lush. Sometimes there is almost no space to move in the woods. The few homes we have seen remind of those we left in the shtetl, simple and serviceable. The farmers are out with their oxen and horses preparing the land for seeds. Our property is perfect. Situated between a river and the forest, we have the land we want to farm and the woods provide not only building materials, but wood to cut to sell to the lumber company so that we can make some money immediately.

This is everything we dreamed of. May you find your Eden as well!"

Simon Adler
Courtesy of the Butler Center for Arkansas Studies, Central Arkansas Library System.

At this a holler went up around the crowd. This commune would make it. It was certainly a better choice than the failed Sicily Island Commune in Louisiana. It was further north so it would not get so hot. The cupboards were raided for vodka to toast the success of the new colony. Moyshe carefully folded the letter and put it back in the envelope that he then nestled in his coat pocket. After the toasts, most the group went to bed. Scheindel and Ruchel went and tucked their children into bed and returned to the table. There three couples met: Moyshe and Ruchel, Mordechai and Sheyndel, and Hirsch and Anna Goodman. The Herders and Woskoboynikoffs knew the Goodmans in Odessa and were amazed when they were on the same ship coming to America. While they were part of *Am Olam*, the Goodmans were not living in the commune. Joining them were a number of single men: Abraham Millner and his two sons Yosef and Zundel, who were not from Odessa but had joined the commune in New York City. There were also Solomon Menaker, Max Goldstein, and David Spies. All told, twenty adults gathered round the table.

Moyshe began, "I think we've found our place."

Abraham Millner asked, "Do we have enough to make the trip?"

One of his twins jumped in the conversation, "More importantly do have money to buy the land?"

The other asked, "What about the tools we need?"

Moyshe began again, "If we have the money, do you like the idea of going?"

There was a resounding positive response. This was what they had come to America to do. As Moyshe had oft repeated: "We come to this country to live like free men and only a farmer can live free."

The next day, he inquired about buying land and what tools they would need. The Hebrew Emigrant Aid Society (HEAS) had helped the group in Arkansas get established by providing them money to buy the land and tools. Moyshe decided the best place to get information was through them.

When he got to their offices he had to wait in the hallway. A board meeting was taking place. There was a huge influx of Jews, and the board was trying to decide how best to distribute their funds to the 14,000 who asked for it. When they finished, Moyshe saw the impeccably dressed banker Jacob Schiff, the well-known Judge Meyer Isaacs, and Jacob Seligman, part of the great Seligman banking family, leave. He had seen images of them in the paper. This inspired great confidence in Moyshe. Such great, powerful, and rich Jewish men helping other Jews fulfill their dreams only meant that these powerful Jews appreciated what agriculture could do for the Jewish people.

Jacob Schiff
Jacob Schiff, A History of Our Time May, 1903, to October 1903, Vol. VI, Doubleday, Page & Co., n.d., 3602.

When he could get into the office, he found the staff quite willing to assist him. The office staff were thrilled to have a group already organized that they could help. *Am Olam* were the people they wanted to help: impoverished Jewish immigrants who were willing to leave the city and become farmers in the West. By moving them west, HEAS hoped to alleviate the over-populated Lower East Side. He was told that timber land was $150 per acre, but they could make a down payment of $25. The rest could come from the sale of the harvested wood. Moyshe believed this to be a good deal and asked HEAS to immediately act upon it. He requested they purchase *Am Olam* some timber and agricultural lands near the group that was already in Arkansas and arrange for transportation. The representative gave Moyshe a list of farm implements and lumbering tools they would need, since Moyshe explained the Odessa *Am Olam* had enough money to purchase their own. Satisfied that he had everything

Judge Myer Samuel Isaacs
Myer Samuel Isaac, The Old Guard and Other Addresses, Knickerbocker Press, 1 January 1906, frontpiece.

arranged, Moyshe promised to return the following week for the tickets and land deed.

On his way home, Moyshe purchased a long rectangular crate in which to store and move the tools he had to purchase. When he got it home, he laid it on the floor in the living room of the main apartment of the commune, which was used as a bedroom.

Gittel watched him curiously and finally pulled on his pant leg and whispered, "Who died, Papa?"

"Whatever do you mean?" he asked.

"You came home with a coffin, so someone must have died."

Moyshe burst out laughing, which made Gittel confused and cry. He took her in his arms to soothe her and said, "Little chick, this is a crate, not a coffin. In it will go all our tools for the farm. We will leave soon and have to get ready."

Gittel looked at him with her large teary eyes, "We are leaving for the farm?"

"Yes, for the farm," he reassured her.

With that she escaped up from his embrace and dashed out of the apartment calling over shoulder, "Wait until I tell the others!"

Over the next few weeks, Moyshe, Mordechai, Hirsch, Abraham, Yosef, Zundel, Solomon, Max, and Abe would bring in tools to deposit in the crate. As chance would permit in their busy schedule, they would purchase hammers and nails, saws, shovels, hoes, and scythes, and other implements. Gittel would stand with her father as he repeated the English names in an attempt to learn them. He wasn't sure what all these tools were for, but had been assured by Michael Heilprin, who had actually dropped off the group's tickets, that each and every one would be required.

9

The Adventure

The day had come and the Herders, Woskoboynikoffs, Millners, and Goodmans, and others to a total of thirty stood in the street outside the tenement they had been living in. For some, like the Herders, they had lived there less than a year. For others, the tenement had been their home for two or three years and had become a substitute for their village in the Old Country. The leave-taking was almost as hard as the last one had been. Before the rest of the commune had gone to bed the night before they had wished their comrades a safe trip and a fruitful farm. Some promised to come join them if they were successful. They didn't get up to wish them off because their sleep was so precious.

The group struggled in the very early morning with their bundles, crates, and the half-asleep children. It was barely 4 am and the streets were dark and empty as they began their hour long trek to the Grand Central Depot to catch their train to St. Louis. They stumbled in the dusky morning through the Lower East Side to 2nd Avenue and then headed north on Cooper Street until it met 4th Avenue. Finally, they reached Union Square Park where they stopped and rested. People took packages of bread out of their bundles. Once breakfast had been consumed, they enjoyed the greenery of the park in the morning light and headed up Park Avenue. The further they trekked, the less urban the road became. The train depot had been built on 42nd Street, which was on the far edge of the city.

Union Square
"Union Square," 1904, New York Public Library Digital Collections, digitalcollections.nypl.org/items/ 510d47e1-06be-a3d9-e040-e00a18064a99.

After over an hour, the group finally reached the depot. Even after a year in one of the grandest cities in the world, they were in awe of the depot. It was huge, over a block long, and had three stories, with towers that made it four or five stories high.

Moyshe gathered the group around him on the steps of the Grand Depot, "I have given you all your own tickets so that if we lose each other in the crowd, you can get to the train. Remember, we are going to some place called Saint Louis. Make sure you get on that train. It leaves at 7 am."

Grand Central Depot, between 1871 and 1898
Grand Central Depot. New York City, New York, Photograph. Library of Congress
www.loc.gov/item/2017658194/

The thirty headed into the building with hundreds of others. The rest of New York City seemed to be packed into this one building. The noise of all those people was deafening. Ruchel grabbed Hannah and Gittel tightly by their hands.

"Stay near, Anna," she warned. "Today is not the day to go exploring."

The single men, who shared carrying their bundles and the crates of tools, moved much quicker than the families and were soon lost in the crowd. Moyshe, was too exhausted and stressed to read the English signs as he still struggled with this new language, wandered among the tracks, stumbling over them as he clutched Saul to his chest with one hand, and holding his bundle with the samovar with the other. Since Ruchel was keeping track of the three girls, she lagged behind.

She looked up and saw a train chugging towards her husband. "Moyshe!!" she cried out in fear.

Moyshe heard her cry and turned to see what upset her. At that moment, he saw the train and jumped out of the way, saving both himself and his son.

Finally, they found their train and their place on it. The Odessa *Am Olam* was again reunited on the train. The group settled in with more than 30 minutes to spare. The children, to whom last year's train trip across Europe seemed a lifetime previous, could not contain their excitement. They were going to travel halfway across the New World! Finally, the conductor came through to check their tickets and the train's whistle blew. Gittel stumbled as the train lurched westward and Zundel caught her before she fell.

The three Herders, the two Woskoboynikoff, and the three Goodman children vied for seats by the windows dashing from one side to the other to see the American countryside pass by. At the various stops, people got on and off the train lugging bundles and suitcases and dragging children. The *Am Olam* children watched families hug and cry in joy as they were reunited. When the conductor stood by the train and called out it was leaving, they watched other families hug and weep as they were being torn apart. While these families joined and broke, women boarded the train with baskets filled with fruit, bread, cans of sardines, and all kinds of other food for sale. People on the train would purchase items to appease their hunger and the vendors would leave before the train left the station. However, when the members of *Am Olam* became hungry, they reached into their bundles for food that they had packed. Heilprin had warned Moyshe, though Moyshe didn't need it, that while food was available at the various stations, it would be very expensive.

When evening fell, everyone admired the sunset over the vast unpopulated America. Then all went dark. The train moved forward unmoved by the vastness of American or the enveloping darkness. The children fell asleep on their parents and all slept through the night. The same thing happened the next day.

Finally, the conductor came through the train announcing their impending arrival in St. Louis. Moyshe stretched and rubbed his eyes. He then awoke his comrades. They checked their bundles and roused the children. Everyone straightened their clothes and smoothed their hair. When the train stopped at the station -- its final destination -- chaos erupted as everyone headed towards the train car exits. Sheindel, Ruchel, and Anna held onto their children in fear that they would be pushed onto the tracks or crushed by the crowd.

St. Louis Train Station
Theodore C. Link, Union Station Building, courtesy of Cotton Belt Route, 1894, Transportation, MHS Photographs and Prints Collection, Missouri History Museum, collections.mohistory.org/resource/111776

During the trip, Moyshe had arranged with his group that those who had carried the crates to the station in New York would go and collect those very crates from the luggage cars and he and the others would find the ticket window for their next train. Everyone would gather there. Thus, when they arrived at 7:00 a.m. in the morning on a bright crisp April morning in St. Louis, the Millners and Max went to the get the crates and the other twenty-six set off to find the ticket office for the Iron Mountain Railway. Heilprin had already obtained their tickets for them, but the location seemed appropriate for a meeting place. Once they had found it, Moyshe sent a few men back to guide the four with the crates and settled everyone in. There were only two hours between the two trains and Moyshe was desperate to make sure they made the connection. Soon enough the weary group saw their comrades toting their crates of tools.

Moyshe previewed his group of future farmers. They were pale and thin from laboring in factories, not on the land. They were excited and exhausted having left their temporary home nearly thirty hours earlier. However, they were all still willing and anxious to start this adventure.

"One more train ride, my friends," he announced cheerily, "and we shall be at our Eden."

Eventually, they made their way to the tracks where their train awaited them. Some of the others boarding the train were traveling all the way to Texas, but the Odessa *Am Olam* were only traveling the first 261 miles. They were getting off at Newport, Arkansas. While the larger portion of the community boarded the train and found their seats, a few of the men had taken the crates to the cargo car. They then fought the crowds to find their fellows and settled in for the next twelve hours.

At 10 minutes after 9 a.m., the whistle blew, the train lurched, and the Odessa *Am Olam* moved closer to its ultimate goal. The children, having spent a whole day on the train, were less enthused by this ride than the last. However, the adults were far more interested. This place they were going was their new home. They watched the plains disappear as they moved into the low mountains of the eastern Ozarks.

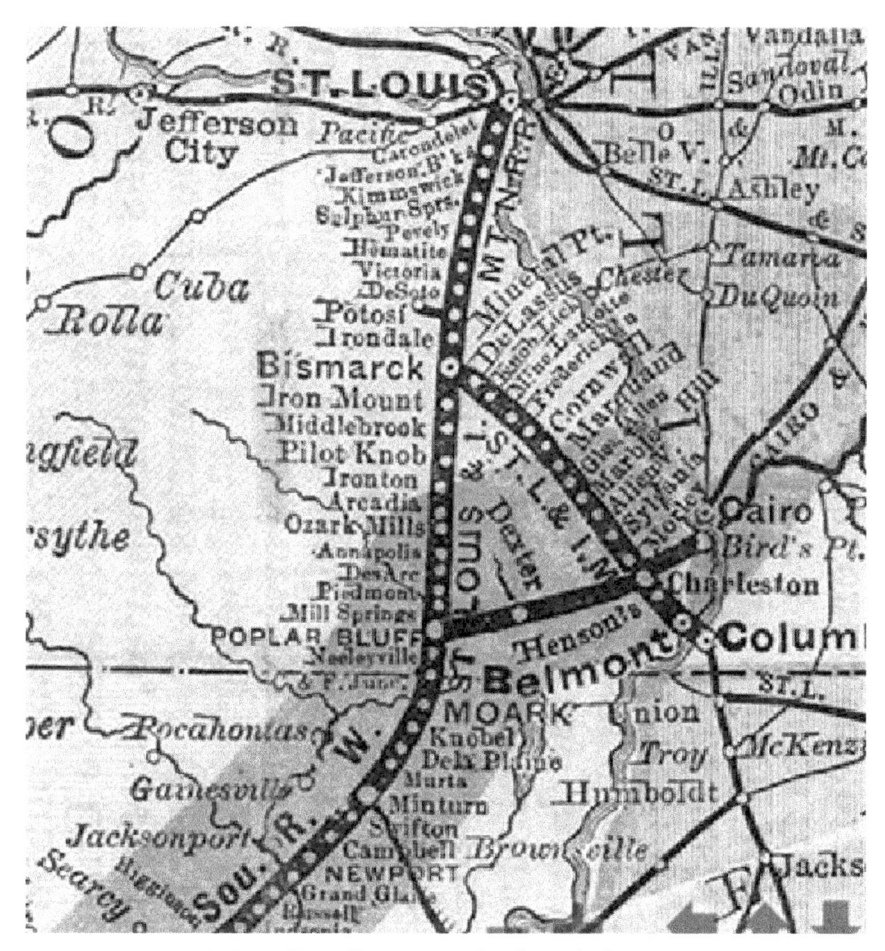

1878 St. Louis Texas Short Line Railroad Broadside: St. Louis to Texarkana

For twelve hours, the train travelled south. It went through forests and up mountains. It crossed and followed the White River many times. The change in geography fascinated the adults. Eventually, the children too renewed their wonder. The trip across Europe had not prepared this group of immigrants for the vast beauty of the New World. Nothing they had heard or read could prepare them for what they saw.

The difference between New York City and St. Louis had been obvious, even with the short time they had been there. The fantastic newly built Grand Depot in New York City was larger than any train station they had ever seen. Union Station in St. Louis was lovely, they all agreed, but nothing like the Grand Depot.

"Where are you taking me?" Ruchel would whisper every once in a while, as she watched the towns go by. While in many respects the villages looked like those in Russia, the distances were huge. Ruchel was frightened by the vastness of the American west.

Pilot Knob
"Bilder Aus Dem Eisenminen-District Unterhalb St. Louis, Missouri." - Scenes From The Iron Mining District Below St. Louis, Um Die Welt, July 15, 1882, Missouri History Museum Collections, mohistory.org/resource/888419.

Anna held her baby to her breast as she commented, "The west is truly as uncivilized as we have heard. There are no towns when we stop."

Her husband, Hirsch, disagreed, "Of course, there are towns. Have you not seen the mail being delivered? If there is a post office, there must be a town no matter how small."

"How is the mail delivered?" asked the younger Hirsch.

The elder Hirsch turned to the boy and stated, "Watch when the train slows. Look backwards, towards the end of the train. There a long wooden arm will swing away from the train towards a man waiting nearby. On the end of the arm is a sack full of mail. He will reach out with a large hook and snag the mail. If we actually stop at a station, the mail is tossed to the side of the track."

As he spoke, the child's eyes grew. "I will watch, very carefully," he promised.

The group's food supplies were growing smaller. Even knowing it would take four days to reach their destination, it was hard to plan how much food they would need because the children could eat so much.

After twelve hours, the train finally arrived at Newport, Arkansas. The group quickly disembarked from the train as it was only staying long enough to reload coal and water. It was just 9 p.m. The sun had just set but there was still light to see by. Their crates seemed to magically appear at the side of the track in the dusk. No one was at the stop except for the thirty members of the Odessa *Am Olam* and the ticket agent. There wasn't even a building to mark the stop.

Street, Newport, Arkansas
Courtesy of Harmon L. Remmel, Jr., late of Fayetteville, Ark.

There was not much to see near the stop. Most stops were on the edge of town and in the semi-dark the area looked deserted. They all looked around and then at each other in confusion. At that moment, the ticket agent reappeared and motioned for the group to follow him.

They did so, having no other place to go. He took them to a large unfinished barn.

"Stay here tonight, you will be safe," he told them, uncertain if anyone understood him. Then he left them to return to his family.

As the group watched him leave, they realized on their own that this barn, or whatever it was, was theirs for the night.

"What is this place?" inquired Max.

Moyshe shrugged his shoulders. "I've no idea, but we have been given this place to stay. Come, let us get the children to bed."

Everyone pitched in. The fresh wood shavings were pushed aside by the new work boots the men had. Moyshe and Scheindel dug through their bundles to find pillows and blankets. With these they covered the carpenters' tables and on these beds the Herder, Woskoboykoff, and Goodman children were put to sleep by their mothers.

As Ruchel prepared Anna, Hannah, Gittel, and Saul for bed, their father searched through the bundles until he found a small one. He carefully opened it and took out the last of their food stores: half a loaf of bread and three cans of sardines.

"Before you sleep, children," he stated as he brought the food to the table, "you should have some supper. Here, eat this." He gave the four, even Saul was now able to eat bread, all that they had left.

"Papa," said Anna, "why don't you have some?"

"Oh, your mother and I will eat later," he replied.

When the children had finished their feast, Moyshe took the three cans and poured the oil from two into the third. Then he took the cord the bundle had been tied with and twisted it into a wick. He stuck it into the can. Then he lit the wick and there was light in the empty space. Moyshe set the make-shift oil lamp on a nearby small table and beckoned Ruchel over. She went and sat down forlornly.

Ruchel was frightened and unhappy. She loved Moyshe deeply, but this place she found herself in was desolate. It had not been clear to either of them, Ruchel or Moyshe, what was ahead. Each move from Odessa to Newport had taken Ruchel further from her normal life. Farming was Moyshe's ideal life, not hers. She just wanted to be with him. Moyshe rifled through the bundles again and found a book he had been secretly carrying. He sat opposite his sad and fearful wife and in the fishy flickering light he read to her. The children only heard the whispers of their father's voice as they fell asleep.

Some of the men went outside. Some simply stared at the stars trying to locate familiar ones. A few had some tobacco and had a slow relaxing smoke, and others went looking for an outhouse or some privacy. It was dark and eerily quiet; at least these men found it so.

"Have you ever heard such silence?" inquired one.

"It is frightening, isn't it?" responded his friend.

"Wait!? Did you hear that?" asked the first.

"A frog?" was the response, "or some odd American creature."

A number of the other men guffawed.

One voice in the dark remarked, "I'm sure there is nothing here that can harm us."

The men finished their evening business and went inside to find a place to sleep.

When the children awoke, the sun was shining low in the sky. Ruchel dressed her brood and the family went out to explore and to let the others sleep.

"Stay near," Ruchel reminded her girls as she picked Saul up.

Hannah dashed here and there dancing in the grass. "Oh, Mamma, look!" she called in delight as she spun in the sun. "The grass goes on and on forever."

"Smell!" countered Anna, "It smells green. Not like the outhouse or dirt. How glorious."

Moyshe and Ruchel smiled at each other. This had been their hope, to raise their children far from industry and the crowds of the cities. The family meandered down the hill away from the barn and came upon a stream. As Moyshe stood guard Ruchel hitched up her dress and had the girls undress. As they did so, Ruchel stripped Saul and bathed them all in the stream.

"Momma," squealed Gittel, "it's cold."

"Cold will not hurt you, but the dirt will," responded their mother.

Soon the girls forgot the cold in the warm sun and splashed in the stream. Saul, too, enjoyed the opportunity to play and splash unrestricted. Ruchel and Moyshe washed their legs and arms and faces. They let the girls run in their underwear in the sun to dry. Moyshe drank deeply of the fresh cold water.

He looked up at his wife. "See what a wondrous Eden this is?" he exclaimed.

Then Moyshe stood and wandered off to see what their daughters were doing.

"Dearest child," asked Moyshe of Gittel when he found her, "What are you doing?"

"Papa," she answered, "my handkerchief was dirty, and I washed it in the stream. Now, I am going to spread it on the grass to dry in the sun."

Moyshe smiled and stroked his daughter's hair. When he looked up, he saw a man on a horse in the distance. He grabbed his hat that had been resting on a tree branch and waved it above his head to get the rider's attention. The rider waved back in acknowledgement and changed his direction to see what Moyshe desired. Moyshe walked towards him. As the children and Ruchel watched, the two men exchanged some words and then the man on his white horse handed Moyshe a small bundle and road off. Moyshe brought the bundle back to his family.

"What was that about?" asked Ruchel.

"I wanted to find out if he was the man who would take us to our farm," he answered. "His accent in English was unfamiliar and with my bad English I do not think we understood each other."

"What did he give you?"

Moyshe grinned broadly and laughed, "He called this his 'tunder.' Let us see what is here." And he sat on the grass with the curious children surrounding him and opened the gift. "A veritable feast! Come, children, sit and I will divide these two rolls and this cheese among you for breakfast."

The hungry children were delighted by the treat and took no notice that their parents had none of the stranger's dinner. When they had finished eating and drinking from the stream, the children put their clothes back on and the family walked back up the hill to the barn. Everyone else was awake, refreshed, and dressed. As people were putting their bedding back into their bundles, two tall thin men riding a covered wagon pulled by two oxen came to the barn.

Covered Wagon with Oxen
Walter T. Oxley, Westward Bound. ca. 1921. Photograph. Library of Congress, www.loc.gov/item/2013648092/.

As leader of the group, Moyshe stepped forward to address them, "You take us to farm?"

The men looked at each other in confusion, not understanding his thick accented bad English. To them it didn't sound like English at all.

Then one stepped forward to shake hands with Moyshe, "Hello. I'm Mike and this is Tom, and we are here to take you out to the farm."

Max stepped up behind Moyshe and whispered in his ear, "What is he saying?"

Moyshe whispered back, "I don't know." He then turned back to the two men, "I am sorry. I do not understand. Is that wagon for our supplies?" And he pointed at the wagon.

Mike faced Tom and said, "This is useless. They don't speak a word of English."

"You're right," Tom answered. "Let's just load 'em up. We've got a long way to travel today."

Then Tom and Mike started tossing bundles up into the wagon. Max and Abe brought forward the crates of tools and four men lifted them up into the wagon. When the other crate was loaded and all the bundles settled, the children were handed up and then Anna, Sheyndel, and Ruchel followed to make sure they were safe.

As the women climbed up, Moyshe returned to the doorway of the barn. There he picked up a good-sized rock that had been used as a steppingstone into the barn. He took something out from under the rock and returned to join everyone else on the wagon.

Hannah turned to Anna and asked, "What was Papa doing?"

"Under the rock?"

"Yes, with the rock."

"Oh," the elder sister answered with some superiority, "he hid the money under the rock so no one would take it."

"Who would take it?" Anna asked confused. "It isn't just Papa's money; it's the group's money."

"He isn't afraid of someone in *Am Olam* taking it. He doesn't know who else is around."

Then Moyshe climbed onto the front of the wagon with Abraham. Everyone else walked behind, mostly relieved that they didn't have to carry anything. Thus, the Odessa *Am Olam* walked towards their new home.

10

The Countryside

Tom and Mike walked on either side of the oxen, chewing twigs from the bushes on the road. Every so often, when their twig didn't taste right, or so the girls thought, they would toss it aside and cut a new one. Every once in a while, one or the other would urge the oxen forward with, "Get up Pencho" and "Get up Fencho."

In the wagon, Anna, Sheyndel, and Ruchel had finally gotten their little ones to sleep nested in the pillows packed in the bundles. Hirsh and Mendel had dozed off, as well. Mendel was curled up in Hirsh's lap. Anna Goodman had gotten her oldest, Friede, to sing to the other children to keep them entertained.

Sheyndel, who had hoped to spend the time doing some mending, sighed, "This isn't half as comfortable as the train. All this bouncing and climbing up hill and rolling downhill. Not even a seat to sit on."

Ruchel reached out to her friend, "Soon there will be no more traveling. Focus on that."

Sheyndel responded with a weak tired smile. The ride continued on. On occasion, one of the children would lift the canvas cover of the wagon to get a glimpse of the outside world. Through the dense green wood, the ox drawn wagon moved forward with nearly twenty men straggling along behind.

All of a sudden, the wagon jolted. Everyone inside tumbled and rolled. Bundles flew in the air and landed with a thump. The two babies, Saul and Sheyndel, awoke screaming.

"Ewwwwwww," swallowed Hannah.

"Disgusting," answered Gittel.

"Mamma," groaned Hirsch. "I feel ill. Breakfast came back."

Sheyndel, too busy trying to organize the bundles back into a safe and balanced pile, answered distractedly, "Swallow hard and get comfortable." Under her breath she continued, "Who knows when this journey will finally end."

Mordechai called out from behind the wagon, "Sheyndel?! Boys?! Are you okay in there?"

Hirsch stuck his head out of the back of the wagon, "Yes, Papa. Can I come out and walk with you?"

"No, my son. We've much farther to walk and your legs just aren't long enough yet."

"Hrumph," responded Hirsch as he pulled his head back inside.

On and on they rolled. Those walking behind the wagon and riding on it had no more idea where they were going than those inside. Not only was the wood dense, but the trees were unfamiliar. These men knew little about the trees in Ukraine and nothing about the trees of the New World. Inside the wagon with the canvas cover, it was impossible to tell the passage of time.

Arkansas Pine Forest
John Hugh Reynolds, Makers of Arkansas History, Silver, Burdett and Co., 1905,
187.

"Shhh...shhhhhhh...," commanded Hannah, "do you not hear that?"
"What?" demanded Hirsch.
"Yes, what?" repeated his little brother.
"I'm not sure," Hannah responded.
"Wait! I hear it too," announced Gittel. "It's not birds."
"Singing?" suggested Anna.
"Not like what I've heard before," responded Friede.
"It's getting louder," stated Gittel.

"Well, clearly we are getting closer," Abraham Goodman retorted.

By now it was clearly identifiable as singing, but none in the wagon could identify the language or the songs. The wagon came to a halt. The children scrambled to the front and back of the wagon to peer out and see what was happening.

Ruchel stuck her head out as well. "What is that?" she wailed. "Is that stack of logs a house?" she asked as she pointed to the log cabin not far from them. Outside the log cabin a group of men and women were sitting singing.

Sheyndel pulled Ruchel back so that she could see. "A log cabin," she whispered in awe. "I thought those were just stories in the newspaper."

Log Cabin
Biographical and Historical Memoirs of Western Arkansas, Southern Publishing Co., 1891, 112A.

Gittel pulled Hannah's braid, "Do you see the funny hats?"

She was referring to the bonnets the women and girls were wearing. The three Herder girls broke out in laughter.

Gittel pulled her *babushka* forward so that her ears were covered in imitation of those girls in front of the cabin singing, "How do they ever hear with their ears covered?"

Again, the Herder girls laughed loudly.

Woman with Bonnet
Acorn Stoves and Ranges. ca. 1886. Library of Congress, www.loc.gov/item/2004666589/.

Tom and Mike dropped the oxen's leads and walked towards the group. The people they were leading were too far away to hear what was said. It would not have much of a difference, since they did not understand English well and the local accent made it almost incomprehensible, and the locals did not know Russian. When the two men finished their greetings, they returned to the immigrants and the oxen.

As the wagon lurched forward, Gittel leaned out the front the wagon to where her father sat, "What was going on there, Papa?"

Moyshe pondered for a moment, "Must be a funeral. The songs were sad and the people were gathered together."

"Thank you, Papa," she responded as she fell back into the wagon when it hit a root.

On went the journey. Sometimes the travelers stopped to eat what crumbs they had left, but mostly onward they went. The oxen did not move swiftly, but their pace was steady. Boredom overcame those in the wagon and so they slept or sang or told each other stories. Because the surroundings were so unfamiliar, the group was unable to gauge how far they had traveled.

Evening had fallen and the sun had left the sky when they finally reached their destination.

"Ho!" cried Moyshe. "We are here at last."

The children scrambled out of the wagon jumping onto the grass before the wagon had even stopped. Tom and Mike halted the wagon and let the two oxen graze. Then they made their way to the back of the wagon. Already members of the commune had helped the women down. Now the two guides helped the men unload all the bundles and crates. They were placed in a pile and then Tom and Mike took the leads of the oxen and climbed up onto the driver's bench on the wagon

Girl wear Babushka
"Photographs Slavic Faces," Teachers of Russia, 2006-2024, www.bolsemir.ru/ index.php?content=text&name-0438&gl=creatfirst.

and turned the wagon around. They went off into the night without even saying goodbye.

The three women stood in front of one of the houses in the clearing. It was not a large house and clearly they were not going to all fit. There were people from the first group of settlers milling around who ran to greet them. Joy filled the air of the existing community. The new arrivals weren't so excited.

"Is that a flight of stairs to get into the house?" Anna Goodman asked hesitantly. "Do you think this is a local custom?"

"At least there is a river nearby," sighed Ruchel.

"Well," said Sheyndel," let us get the children to bed and worry about what we cannot change tomorrow. I'm too tired to talk with anyone."

They gathered the children and took them to the river to wash their faces and feet. Then they traipsed back to the clearing for a meal of whatever the settlers had to spare. When the meal was over, the women unpacked the bundles containing bedding and made beds for the children and themselves. After a series of questions and answers down in the clearing, the men unpacked their sleeping materials. Soon around them all that could be heard were crickets chirping and frogs croaking.

White River
John Hugh Reynolds, Makers of Arkansas History, Silver, Burdett, 1905, 85.

11

The New Day

When Gittel awoke in the morning, she snuck through the room that was the house and down the stairs. There was no chamber pot, so she had to find somewhere to relieve herself. When she got to the bottom of the stairs, she discovered all the men sleeping on the ground.

Yosef sat up, "Little one, what are you doing here so early?"

She looked at him desperately and stared off into the woods with trepidation. Yosef untangled himself from his blanket and slipped on his boots. Then he stood up and bleary-eyed took Gittel's hand.

"All you need is a tree," he commented. "So, let's find you one." And they walked away from the houses and the clearing it sat in. When they found a spot Yosef thought was suitable, he left Gittel there and walked a few paces away and turned his back. "Now, child, you do your business and come here when are done. It's a good thing, I guess, that we all couldn't fit in the house. Otherwise, who would have been around to take you here?" He paused as he looked at the grand trees he was surrounded by and then continued his meandering monologue, "You know, we are going to have to learn the names of these trees." He chuckled, "And how to how to cut them down." Then a child's trusting hand slipped into his and he stopped chatting. He looked down into the deep brown eyes of a trusting seven-year-old. "You are ready to return to Mamma?" he inquired.

"Yes, and thank you," Gittel replied in a tiny voice.

Together they walked back to the clearing where some of the other men where just starting to awaken. One was just returning from the river with a bucket of clean water, and a few wandered back from other parts of the woods.

"Off to Mamma," Yosef directed as he left her at the bottom of the stairs.

Gittel dutifully complied. She found this wild new place frightening, and she was hungry. When she climbed into the house, Gittel discovered her mother, and the others were awake. The women were in deep discussion over the food. The previous night, Moyshe had taken one corner of the house and had everyone put their food there. Now the three women were trying to plan their meals for as long as they could because no one had any idea when their crops would come in and the lumber cutting would profit. Anna had her baby on her breast and Hirsch, Mendel, Abraham, and Isaac Goodman were chasing each other around the house leaping over those who were half asleep.

Then from down below Moyshe called up, "Come down! Everyone else is awake."

Ruchel left Saul with her Anna. Sheyndel and Anna Goodman went downstairs to meet everyone else.

One of the men came forward with a large sack and dropped it at their feet, "We don't have much. This is pretty much it. A sack of corn meal, but that should help us all right now."

Max took the sack and threw it over his shoulders and lugged it upstairs to the hoard of food, so that the women could dole it out as appropriate. Then the men began discussing what the plans were for the whole commune, now that the new arrivals were ready to start work.

A few of the men built a fire and some of the others went down to the river with buckets to collect water. Ruchel came downstairs with a bowl full of corn meal and Sheyndel followed with a skillet and Mendel. When the men returned with the water, Ruchel added water to the meal. When the skillet that had been placed over the fire was hot, Ruchel dropped in some fat. When that had melted, she placed corn meal patties in the skillet and turned them as they browned with a fork. When done, she handed them to whomever put out a hand for breakfast. All the while, Moyshe and some of the others made plans to start work for the day.

Solomon, one of the few with farming experience, as he had been at the defunct Sicily Island commune, raised concerns, "This does not bode well. Has no one wondered why the house stands on stilts like a bath house at the sea?"

"What does it mean?" asked Zundel curiously.

"I believe," Solomon responded, "that this area floods regularly. This can be a serious problem."

"Where does this leave us?" Max called out from the back of the crowd.

"Deeply in debt," answered Moyshe sadly. "We have no money for tickets back to New York City, or even St. Louis, and we owe much on the timber land."

"So," Abe interjected, "We give up our dream of farming and become, what is the word?"

"Lumberjacks," Yosef jumped in.

"Yes, we become lumberjacks," Abe finished.

"We are stuck here," Moyshe commented despondently. "We are stuck here for at least nine months. Hopefully, by then we can at least pay off our debt."

"What then do we do?" Zundel asked.

"Well," Moyshe pondered, "We unpack the saws and leave the scythes and shovel in the crates."

With Moyshe's pronouncement, the crowd of about 30 wandered off to wash, to eat, and to accept their situation.

Ruchel approached Moyshe despondently, "You see the reality of this place. I am here because of my love for you. There is much I will suffer to be with you, but I cannot live in that house with all those people and not you. Please, we must have our own home."

Moyshe took her in his arms and pulled her close. He whispered a promise in her ear, "I will do my best to make us a home."

A few days later the actual owner of the houses arrived to check on everyone. He was a short broad man named Ellery, or so the community came to believe.

"Moyshe," said Ellery, "I have a proposition for you."

"Oh?" Moyshe raised an eyebrow and the two walked off deep in discussion.

Some of the men had gone off to the woods to cut some trees. The women had taken the children to play and to wash the clothes.

When the day ended and all were in bed, whether in the house asleep or camped out in the clearing, Moyshe and Ruchel sat on the bottom steps of the stairs to the house where Ruchel was sleeping. They held hands and looked up at the stars.

"Mr. Ellery has given us a way to earn some food. He wants us to cut the bushes and lower branches away from the tall trees so that later his sons can cut the trees. Then we are to gather all this brush and make it into piles."

"What do we get in exchange?" asked his wife.

"Cows, horses, pigs, matches, corn meal, and the whey from his cheeses," responded Moyshe.

"Well, this certainly is not what we intended when we came here," commented Ruchel, "but the work is honest and the food welcome. I don't believe we have much of a choice."

"No," agreed Moyshe, "But we are here and will make the best of it. Now, we must go to bed." They kissed goodnight and Ruchel mounted the stairs to the children safe above, while Moyshe unrolled his blanket under the stars.

12

The Home Coming

Moyshe had left early in the day to meet some local men. They were busy building a house for Ruchel. The other men were off doing their best to add to the slowly growing pile of trains ties. All the children were playing in the clearing. Hirsch and the Goodman boys, Abraham and Isaac, were climbing trees. Hannah and Friede Goodman were watching the younger children. Anna and Gittel had been charged with cleaning the house and the clearing. At the edge of the clearing, they started collecting hickory nuts.

"Silly," laughed Anna, "hold out your apron like I have." And she nudged her little sister to get her attention.

Gittel dropped her two handfuls of nuts into Anna's apron and lifted her own apron up with one hand. The two continued deeper into the woods. They were enchanted by the light and shadow play caused by the sun and leaves above. They couldn't see the birds singing around them and even if they could, they wouldn't have been able to identify them. The birds here were different than the ones back home. In the distance a chickadee chanted.

Blue Jay
The Blue Jay. 1880. [Augusta, Maine: Published by True & Co. Augusta Maine] Library of Congress, www.loc.gov/item/2003690936/.

"Look! Look!" squealed Gittel.

"What? Where?" her sister responded breathlessly.

"Something bright blue flew through the trees."

"Oh, really? Let's see if we can get closer." And off the girls trotted holding their aprons carefully so as not to drop their nuts.

After a few minutes, they stopped. "Did you see it again?" Anna asked her sister in hushed tones.

"No," Gittel responded sadly.

"Oh well," Anna sighed. "Well, we should get back."

"Ok. Which way is home?" asked a confused Gittel.

"Oh no, I'm not sure," her sister replied with a panicked tone. "Wait, I hear something."

"Yes, a hammer. Someone is building," agreed Gittel.

"Let's go there," declared Anna. In their haste to find their way home, they dropped their nuts and walked quickly towards the persistent pounding.

In a clearing much like their own, they found a lone man building a house. Anna and Gittel looked at each other in wonderment. For a few moments, they stood in the shadows at the edge of the clearing watching this stranger construct his home. They had not thought others were here in the wilderness living like them. Gittel nudged Anna and Anna shook her head "no." They stood a few more minutes. Gittel nudged Anna again. Anna took a deep breath, took a step forward, and hesitated. Gittel took a step forward, as well. There they were a step out of the shadow of the woods. Anna looked down at her little sister and strode forward.

"Excuse me?" she asked hesitantly in strongly accented English. "Excuse me," she announced.

The man looked up. To his surprise, two little girls were there. He smiled gently and asked, "What can I do for you?"

The girls were not exactly sure what the man said, since they knew little English and his accent wasn't familiar, but he sounded friendly.

"Sir," Anna pleaded, "we are lost and do not know the way home."

The man looked at them and realized he did not understand them because of their strong accent. He thought for a moment and then he realized who they were, "You are part of that group of Russian Jews aren't you? Are you lost?"

"We are lost," Anna replied, not realizing she had answered the man's question.

"Well, it won't be hard to get home from here," he answered as if he knew what she had said. "Just turn right around and walk straight through the woods and you'll get home again." And he gestured them back in the direction they had come.

Anna and Gittel looked at each other and turned around and walked as directed. The man had been very clear in his motions. They ignored the sweet scent of the pine trees and the powerful hickory trees and focused on just getting home. The crows taunted them to no avail. These girls were on a mission. Rather than listening to the tapping of the woodpecker, they stayed true to their course.

After an unbeknownst time, they arrived home. No one had realized they were missing. The boys were done climbing trees and were busy with a game of catch using an old apple. The girls were still busy watching the little ones. Anna gave Gittel a warning look and Gittel raised her eyebrows, and no one ever heard the story.

13

The Spring

The hard work of cutting lumber had become real to these urban men. The men were not physical laborers by trade. They were teachers and factory workers. No one had warned them of the exertion they had to sweat through. The men grew blisters large and painful that turned into callouses. This was something new, as their callouses had come previously from tight boots and writing quills.

First the men had experimented and discovered the pine trees to be much easier to cut. The wood was much softer than the hickory. However, soon enough they discovered that the sticky pine sap destroyed their saws. They spent the evenings scraping that sticky goo off their equipment, which was almost impossible.

Then they turned to the hickory trees. These were just as tall and straight as the pine, but the wood was immensely harder. It could take a day or more to fell a single tree and then it had to be cleaned of limbs and cut into logs a certain length. This could last two or more days for just one tree. The men grew despondent that their vision of a glorious agricultural life had not come to fruition. They needed one thousand staves to earn $20. It took a pair of men two weeks to produce such an order. However, they only received half the payment. The other half was paid when Mr. Stevely, the owner of Newport Lumber, received the staves.

Lumber Company, Newport
Fay Hepmstaed, A Pictorial History of Arkansas: From Earliest Times to the Year 1890, N. D. Thompson Pub., 1890, 990.

Life had to continue. The woman began to prepare for Passover.

Hannah turned to Mendel and asked, "Did you hear our mothers whispering?"

"Yes, what about?" he asked her.

"I don't know. I thought you did. We need to ask the older kids what is '*matzah*'[12]," she answered.

They wandered toward the river where they knew Hirsch and Anna had been sent to get water. The path between the clearing and the river was well worn by now. Halfway there, they came upon Anna and Hirsch walking towards them.

Hirsch was feeling quite manly as he was given chores rather than being left to play. "What do you want, children?" he asked haughtily.

"Brother," began Mendel, "What is '*matzah*'? Mamma keeps talking about."

"A kind of bread," she responded and continued past.

"Well, not exactly," corrected Anna. "It is hard and crunchy, like..."

Hirsch put his buckets down and turned, "like three day old really thinly sliced bread."

"How can bread be three days old?" inquired the little boy.

Anna laughed, "You are too little to remember when we had extra food." Hannah looked at her sister curiously. Anna handed the younger two one of her buckets and walked quickly towards Hirsch. "Let me help you," she called. The two walked together with a bucket between them and a bucket on the other side.

When they returned to the clearing. They found their mothers busy making a dough of the little wheat flour the community had. Their mothers then made flat thin patties with this dough and baked it in the oven. While usually they encouraged the girls to help with the kitchen duties, this time they told them to stay back. There was no extra flour and time was of the essence. The dough could not sit for than five minutes before it had to be baked. Once baked, they were carefully wrapped in a clean cloth and put away in a trunk for safe keeping.

Two days later all the children were dragged to the river for a wash. Rather than protest, like they might have had they been shown a bathtub, the children rejoiced.

"Swimming," called out Saul and hoots and hollers rang in the clearing as the children dashed down to the river. Saul toddled after them. Sheyndel, Ruchel, Anna and the other mothers followed behind with the laundry, washing boards, and soap.

Once there, Ruchel admonished Anna and Hannah, "Daughters, you must wash and watch the little ones."

"Everyone," Sheyndel announced, "Down to your underclothes and into the river."

The children whooped and cheered as they tossed their clothes aside and stormed the river. Anna took the now naked littlest Goodman, Sheyndel, and Hannah took Saul with them into the water. While the children splashed, the women found rocks upon which to pound the clothes and rest their washboards. They even undressed to their underclothes to wash their dresses and aprons. They hung the clothes on the nearby bushes and low branches and lay them on the warm grass. Then they joined the children in the river to wash and to save the littlest ones from the passionate play of the older ones.

White River, Newport
Carol M. Highsmith, Overview of the White River in Newport, Arkansas. United States Arkansas Newport Jackson County, 1920. Library of Congress, www.loc.gov/item/2020741861/.

After an hour or so, the women dragged the children out to dry on the banks in the sun. There Ruchel told them a story to them occupied.

"Long, long ago before there was a United States or a Russia or even Jews in Europe," began Ruchel mysteriously.

"There was never a time without the evil czar," retorted Hirsch.

"Oh, there was," Ruchel answered, "only there was a king called Pharoah and he wasn't any better. He made slaves of the Jews. They worked harder under him than the Jews suffered under the czars of Russia." Now all the children sat silently enthralled; their parents had made the czar into the most evil person alive. "Finally, the Pharoah's hate for the Jews grew to the point where he demanded all the boy babies be killed. He was terrified that the Jews might try to overthrow him." Saul ran to his mother, who put him in her lap while she continued. "But one mother could not bear for such a thing to happen and after her son was born she wrapped him carefully and put him in a waterproof basket and put the basket on the river Nile."

"Is this the Nile?" asked Isaac.

"Shhhhh, silly," whispered Anna, "we aren't in Egypt, so this isn't the Nile."

"But she was scared for her son, so the mother sent her daughter, the baby's big sister, to watch from the river's edge to see what happened to the baby," continued Ruchel. "Miriam watched, that's the sister's name, as the Pharaoh's daughter took the baby out of the Nile and named him Moses. When Moses grew up he didn't know he was a Jew. He also didn't like that the Jews were slaves and were beaten by the Egyptians. So, he ran away from the family he knew."

"The Pharaoh's family," interjected Gittel.

"Yes, right," her mother nodded, "and went into the desert to hide and think."

"Is this a desert?" asked Isaac again.

Anna Goodman giggled, "No, little goose, a desert is a place filled with sand that has no water. We've had rain here and look at the plants. Deserts have no plants."

Ruchel went on, "In the desert he found a bush on fire and it spoke to him. It was God speaking through that fire. God didn't like how his people were being treated and he told Moses how to save his people. He also told Moses that Pharaoh's family was not his family and where to find his real sister Miriam. And so Moses went back to the city and found Miriam and met his brother Aaron and told them of God's plan to save the Jews. Miriam and Aaron, of course, agreed to help Moses. And after much arguing with Pharaoh that included God sending ten plagues to the Egyptians,..."

Once more that Goodman child interrupted and asked, "What were those plagues?"

Ruchel began, "Locusts that ate the crops, boils that killed the cows."

"Frogs that infested everything," added Sheyndel.

"And the water turned to blood," the child's mother added.

"Only the last one I remember," and here Ruchel paused for dramatic effect and then continued in a loud whisper, "The death of the firstborn son! With this last plague, Pharaoh ordered Moses to take the Jews out of Egypt. He did. The Jews left the very next morning. They packed so quickly that the mothers baked their bread before it rose."

"So that's '*matzah*'!" Mendel called out, "bread before it rose."

"Yes," laughed his mother.

"The Jews marched toward the Red Sea carrying all they owned believing that Moses would save them. And Moses marched at the front of them like a general with his sister and brother behind him. But Pharaoh now realized what he had done. He had given up his labor force and shown himself to be a weak leader. He was angry. He called his generals." And Ruchel's voice had grown louder as she told this part, "and sent them with their horses and chariots after the Jews. Pharaoh wanted his slaves back!" Ruchel stopped to catch her breath and grab a handkerchief that the wind had set free from a bush.

"What happened?" demanded Gittel.

"The Pharaoh's army with their horses and chariots chased after the Jews. The Jews saw them coming but were at the Red Sea without a boat. Moses raised his walking stick," and here Ruchel stood Saul up, put a twig in Saul's hand, and raised it high turning Saul into Moses. "And called out to God for help. God answered by splitting the Red Sea like the part in Hannah's hair and all the Jews walked to the other side safely on dry land. But when the Pharaoh's army tried to use the same path, God pushed the water back together and washed them away. And so the Jews were saved from being Pharaoh's slaves."

"Hurrah," shouted Saul.

And everyone repeated his call, "Hurrah!"

"Now," Sheyndel interrupted, "that we are clean and mostly dry, we need to get dressed so that we can return home and celebrate this great victory."

The children were so excited they dashed madly around collecting their clothes. The merry gathering folded the rest of the damp clothes and gathered the remaining soap and wash boards. Hirsch mounted

Saul, who was still holding his twig high, on his shoulders and led everyone on a march home.

When the troupe got back to their home, the three mothers joined Mrs. Goldstein in the preparations for the evening. In no way could the entire community gather in any of the structures in the clearing, so the older children were tasked with assembling the smaller tables into one large on in the center of the clearing. In an effort to recreate the Passover ceremony as closely as they could in their poverty, Mrs. Goldstein had gathered nuts and chopped them and added some apple bits and mixed it all together with some jam that she had discovered. This would stand, the women had agreed, for the *charoset* traditionally made of apples, walnuts, and wine that represented the mortar the Hebrew slaves used to build for the Egyptians. For the traditional bitter herb, the children had collected wild onion grass. One child had picked up an animal bone while playing and so that would suffice for the representation of the sacrifice. The best they could do for a green leaf to represent the spring harvest was to use dandelion, which they had discovered was edible. One of the men had traded a farmer for some eggs, so while there was no way to have the traditional feast, at least, the community agreed, they could have the ceremony.

As evening began to fall, the men returned via the path from the river. They had all stopped to clean themselves. Mrs. Goldstein had found a clean sheet and spread it over the tables. The women had dressed themselves and the children in their best clothes. Everyone came forward to the table where the women had placed bowls and plates of the required food to celebrate Passover.

"Wait!" called out Max, "Where is the wine?"

"Moyshe," Abe asked, "weren't you going to get the wine?"

"Yes, but," Moyshe responded, "we didn't have the money to have it shipped in. There isn't any to be had around here."

"Then what do we do?" asked Max.

"Perhaps we could substitute coffee?" suggested Mordechai.

"Ruchel," Moyshe turned to his wife, "would you bring a pot of coffee and a mug?"

Ruchel dashed off to one of the houses to get a pot of coffee. When she returned with a mug and the pot of warm coffee, the children gathered around Moyshe to see what would happen. How could this strange combination of food help celebrate the wondrous Moses in the story?

The women gathered together and lit two precious candles. Together they chanted the ancient blessing that welcomed a holiday. A hush fell over the community. This was the first holiday they were celebrating as a community in the New World.

But when Moyshe raised the mug of coffee to bless the "wine," the spell was broken. The emotional stress of being in the wilderness in an unknown place, attempting a new way of living, and being in poverty had been hard, but cobbling together an attempt at a Passover Seder was just too much. Mrs. Goldstein broke down in tears.

"This isn't right," she sobbed. "We need wine and roast chicken and..."

Her husband had to gently take her away and put her to bed. The magic, however, was broken. Even the children now saw that this was a poor copy of what should be. Moyshe plowed through the ceremony as best he could remember. He introduced the children to the sadness represented by the bitter wild onion, the ancient rites that the animal bone and roasted egg stood for, the slaver showed by the nuts mixed with apples and jam. He talked to them about the joy Jews found in wine and the purpose of the four cups of wine Jews are required to drink during the ceremony. They all partook of the *matza* and remembered their ancestors who had fled the land of Egypt for freedom. By the time the ceremony was over, the children felt a new respect for their Jewishness. They went to bed humbled on that April night.

14

The Rains

"How soon," Ruchel asked Moyshe on day over their meager breakfast of corncakes, "are we going to makemoney?"

"Are things that desperate?" her husband inquired.

"Our food supplies are low, we have no more soap, the children are outgrowing their clothes, and most of the men need new clothes and boots. Yes, we are desperate."

"The trees are harder to cut than we thought. I never knew that there was so much skill involved in cutting a tree. Did you know that one should take the limbs off first and one should saw them from the underside up?"

Ruchel looked at him blankly. Her mind was filled with the very practical day-to-day needs of the community.

Moyshe continued without noting her frustration, "We have only gotten paid half for each log when it is cut. To get the other half we have to get the logs to Mr. Wiysel in Newport. We've had to pay the mortgage. I don't know how we will get out of this mess."

Ruchel became very practical, "How do we get these few logs to Wiysel?"

"We've been told that we float them there," Moyshe answered. "But we just don't have enough yet." He looked at his wife in despair.

Log Float
Logging in the alluvial lands of the Mississippi River. Cotton plantation in the Arkansas River Valley. Arkansas River Valley Mississippi River, 1901. Library of Congress, www.loc.gov/item/91796526/.

"I will do what I can to stretch the supplies," Ruchel answered despondently.

Then they looked at each other curiously. The smell in the air had changed. Hesitantly, they took each other's hand and looked up. Through the trees in the distant sky, they saw grew clouds gathering.

"Only a rainstorm," Moyshe commented trying to be nonchalant.

"Maybe it will help cool down the air," Ruchel added hopefully. "No matter, I'll go take down the laundry."

"I'll get some help to get the firewood covered."

The two went to organize the camp before the rain came. Most of the men were off in the woods working in teams to cut trees. They had left in the morning half-light and would be back before the sun was high. It was just too hot to work during the afternoon. Moyshe gathered the children and they worked to move the wood under the houses on stilts.

The sky got greyer and greyer until the rain finally came. There was no lightning and thunder, just a steady constant rainfall for hours. The

Am Olam found it to be a respite from the heat and enjoyed the fresh smell. After a few hours, the storm passed. The men returned from the woods and unrolled their wet bedding under the shady trees to wait out the heat.

When the steamy afternoon subsided, the men decided it was time to go back to work. It had only taken a few days for the habit of shaking out boots to take hold. Gittel giggled as she watched all the men turn their boots over and shake out the snakes and bugs that had taken refuge from the storm and the heat. Their bedding had gotten no drier laying on the wet ground. Before returning to work, they hung their bedding from the branches of the trees surrounding the clearing.

Sheyndel remarked with a great sigh, "Who would have thought we'd live in the midst of a laundry?"

Hirsch laughed so hard at his mother's comment that he rolled off the step he was sitting on. This set off his little brother. Unfortunately, the two were now covered in mud. The clearing was now soggy with muddy puddles everywhere.

"Boys," commanded their mother, "go down to the river and wash yourselves and your clothes."

Hirsch grabbed Mendel's hand and trudged off. They quickly returned.

"Mamma," Hirsch called, "the river is flooded. There's no bank anymore. It's a swamp."

The three women looked at each other in fear. Sheyndel ran to gather her sons.

"You stay away from the river until it isn't swollen any longer," she whispered in their ears.

Ruchel turned her back on everyone so they would not see her reaction to the boys' news. Without a swift flowing river, the logs could not be towed to Newport. If the logs were not delivered, there would be no money, there would be no more food. She felt hopeless and angry and frustrated. Taking a deep breath, she hid her concerns and put on a smooth, unconcerned face before she turned back to her friends.

"Let us find some barrels and fill them with all the clean water we can find," Ruchel began. "Then we can wash the children and consider supper."

Anna went into one house and Ruchel the other, while Sheyndel set out to find a barrel in the area they mockingly named a shed. Anna and Ruchel were not surprised to find pots and boxes filled with water. No one was convinced that the roofs were watertight, and the condition of the houses proved their suspicions. Carefully, they carried the water filled vessels down to the barrel Sheyndel had moved to the base of the stairs to one of the houses.

"I had hoped," Anna said, "that the rain would cool the air."

"Clearly, that didn't happen," Ruchel responded as she wiped the sweat running down her forehead.

After they had filled the barrel, Sheyndel took a cupful out and a rag and did her best to wipe her children down with the water. Ruchel looked at their dwindling food supply and decided on corn cakes for supper.

The community continued on for the next few days in relative peace. Everyone was cranky from the excessive heat, over 100° F, and the humidity and lack of food. The community only ate two meals a day now in an effort to stretch the dwindling food supply. Then the mosquitos attacked.

The incessant buzzing made life unbearable. People became angry slapping themselves to stop the endless biting and whining. Everyone was covered in welts from the bites. The best treatment they had was mud. So where before people had spent time at the river trying to clean themselves of the mud, now they purposely slathered themselves with mud. Cleanliness was nearly impossible. Desperation was setting in, but everyone held on to hope. Things had to get better. The rains would end. The heat would dissipate. The river will return to its banks and the logs would get to the lumber yard and then there would be money for food.

15

The Fever

Two weeks later, after the on-and-off rain showers only made the heat more unbearable and the clearing was like living on the edge of a swamp, it began. A few of the men complained of chills and muscle aches. Ruchel had them brought into one of the houses. At least they would be off the damp ground. She spent her time trying to fight the chills and fever with cool water. There was nothing else she could do. Soon more men came down with the fever and even the children developed the fever. It took only two days for at least a third for the community to come down with the fever. Moyshe sent Yosef to town for a doctor.

"You seem the least affected by this illness," he announced. "so, you need to go."

"You are probably right," Yosef answered. "I just have a headache and a mild fever. I'll leave now and come back with a doctor."

Ruchel threw a question over shoulder as she squatted over a chamber pot, "How will we pay this good doctor?"

"Wife, ever practical wife," answered Moyshe, "First let us get well and then we can figure that out." Then he turned to Yosef, "Be safe and good luck."

Yosef left the clearing headed on the path to the road to Newport. As he did so, some more men of the community stumbled back to the clearing. A few were doubled over supported by their friends. Yosef waved at them sadly and trudged on. Those left behind who could stand helped settle in the newly arrived sick.

Almost seven hours later, those who could turned towards the road. They heard the sound of horses' hooves on the ground. In rode a well-dressed healthy man on a brown horse with Yosef just hanging on. As the horse slowed, the stranger looked around him assessing the situation. It didn't take much for him to know what was happening. He saw a hundred pale undernourished people laying on soggy ground. As the horse stopped, the stranger gracefully dismounted and caught Yosef before he fell off the horse. Abraham stumbled forward to take his son and greet the doctor.

The doctor put his hand out and introduced himself, "Hello, I'm Dr. Heard."

By now most of the men had had enough exposure to their neighbors to have developed the most basic of English skills. "Hello, I Abraham Millner, Doktur."

"I came as fast as I could. I'm terribly glad that Yosef came to get me. You get him settled comfortably and I'll have a look around," Dr. Heard commanded.

Abraham was not exactly sure what the doctor had said, but he understood the intent. He hustled his son to the patch under one of the great pine trees that the father and sons had made theirs. He tucked Yosef in next to his twin Zundel and wandered off to find the doctor.

All this time, the doctor had walked his horse to one of the houses and tied him to a strut and then he dashed up the stairs with his doctor's bag in his hand. He stopped and checked on each person in the house. Ruchel, hunched and quaking over her children as she tried to cool their fevers with a cool damp rag, eyed the stranger skeptically. He came up to her and squatted.

"Hello, my dear," he smiled. "I'm Doctor Heard. Yosef came to get me." He had no idea how much English she knew, but he hoped that a cheery and calming voice would win her over. He saw her pale complexion, felt the heat of her fever, and could smell she suffered from diarrhea. He looked at her children and saw the same. "I know exactly what ailment this is. The treatment is effective and absolutely painless." He could tell from her demeanor that he was making headway. She relaxed and followed his movements with her eyes. The word "doctor" had registered in her understanding. "Madam, show me where you've some coffee and we can begin."

She wasn't sure why he wanted coffee, but she had not forgotten how to be hospitable. "Come, come," she waved after she stood shakily and took him downstairs after grabbing a small canvas sack. Still shivering, she led him to a fire with a pot of water boiling over it. Into this pot, she threw some handfuls of ground coffee and waited for the aroma to waft over them both.

Heard was impressed with her attitude. As ill as she was, this woman continued on. Nothing was going to beat her down. When the coffee was done, Ruchel dipped a mug in and handed the doctor a mug of boiling coffee. He smiled and took a packet from his bag. He ripped it open and shook a white powder into the coffee. After swirling the coffee around, he handed it back to Ruchel, "Drink this."

Ruchel looked at him skeptically and shook her head, "No."

"It's medicine. Trust me."

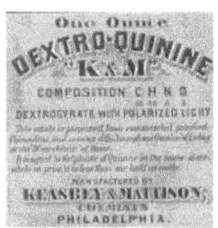

Quinine label
Trademark registration by Keasbey & Mattison for Dextro-Quinine "K&M" brand Medicinal Preparation. 1879. Library of Congress, www.loc.gov/item/2022669031/.

Since she realized she had little choice as nothing she was doing was helping, Ruchel hesitantly took the coffee and sipped it. It didn't taste any different and so she drank it all.

"Good," the doctor said as he patted her on her shoulder. "Now we have to give everyone here the medicine," he said as he passed his arm around the clearing.

"*Da!*[13] *Dabro!*[14]" Ruchel replied and meandered off to find more mugs after she realized this powder was a medicine.

When she'd found a number of mugs, she returned. Dr. Heard showed her his supply of quinine and together they filled mugs with coffee, poured in quinine, swirled, and took these mugs off to the people laying around. When their mugs were empty, they returned and repeated the process. They did not even think of washing the mugs between uses. These two were desperate to get the medicine into everyone before someone died.

Once everyone had had a mug of coffee, the doctor and Ruchel sat down. They both heaved a huge sigh and held hands. Slowly smiles spread across their faces. They had done it. Ruchel then went upstairs to bed. The doctor went to his horse and took down his bedroll. He had known when he left Newport he would have to spend the night. After finding a comfortable spot in the clearing, the doctor spread out his blanket, took off his boots, and went to sleep.

In the morning as the group awoke, the doctor started his rounds. Already some of the *Am Olam* members were feeling better. As he talked to the people, the doctor discovered some of them spoke a bit of English and so he could get some questions answered.

"Why is everyone covered in patches of mud?" was the first question he asked.

Abe answered, "bumps itch."

The doctor went back to his horse and dug through the saddle bag. He found a tin and went to the barrel of water. There he wetted a rag and finally returned to Abe. Gently he wiped off the spots of mud off Abe.

"Which ones itch?" he asked as he opened the tin. As Abe pointed out the bites that still itched, the doctor spread a bit of the paste in the tin on the spot. When he had finished with Abe, the doctor closed the tin and licked his finger.

Abe looked at him curiously, "Good?"

"Actually, yes. Its blackberry paste." The doctor opened the tin and offered it to Abe.

Abe sniffed it cautiously and then stuck his finger in. After tasting the end of this finger, he nodded his head and agreed, "Good."

The doctor smiled. Ruchel and Sheindel came downstairs with coffee and corncakes.

Ruchel handed the doctor a mug of coffee and a cake. "*Spaseeba*,[15]" she said hoping that this meager breakfast would suffice.

Then she slapped herself and started to scratch. The doctor came over with the tin of blackberry paste. He opened it and applied a small dab to Ruchel's growing welt. Then he handed the tin to Ruchel.

"Here," he said gently, "for the bug bites."

She smiled in thanks and took the tin.

He sat down and picked up the mug and corncake and enjoyed his breakfast. When he finished, he went back to his horse and removed the saddle bags. These bags were filled with all kinds of medicine that the doctor traveled with because he never knew what he would need. Finally, after digging around he found what he wanted. It was one of the larger tins in his collection. Carefully, he put everything back in the saddle bags and slung them back over the horse. He turned to find Ruchel. She was on the far side of the clearing applying the paste to the children. He strode over with the tin in hand.

"Ruchel," he announced holding the tin to her in two hands.

She took the tin and almost dropped it. It didn't look like it weighed a full pound. She looked at him quizzically.

"It's quinine for the fever." Then he produced a spoon with a tiny cup from his pants pocket. "One of these spoonfuls in a mug of coffee everyone day for everyone." He took the spoon and banged it on a mug.

"*Da*," She responded. Then she hung her head, "no money."

"That's okay, pay when you can," he answered. He went off to check on the rest of the people. After checking on everyone, he felt assured that the people were improving. He sought out Moyshe.

"Mr. Herder," he began, "Send for me whenever there is a problem. Everyone should be getting better. And pay when you can with what you have. I'll come back in a week or so to check on you."

Moyshe was not totally sure what the doctor had said, but he shook the doctor's hand and responded, "Tanks."

Then the doctor mounted his horse and rode back to Newport.

16

The Recovery

Ruchel was dutiful in her medication distribution. Every morning, she put one dose in everyone's cup of coffee. After three days most people started to feel better and two days later those people were back to work. Some of the rest took longer to heal.

On the fifth day, Dr. Heard came back. This time he came with a wagon of supplies. The children ran to greet him with cheers. He was something of a hero to them. He handed Hirsch a bag of candies.

"Share with everyone," he commanded.

Hirsch was not exactly sure what the doctor said, but he knew the rules. All the children stood around him as he untwisted the top of the paper bag. Candies were unheard of among this group. At first, they stood around Hirsch staring at the precious gift. The shiny sugary treats in greens, beiges, and pinks were mesmerizing. Mendel, who had little patience, stuck his hand in the bag and took out one piece of candy. The children watched him in wonderment as he popped the treat into his mouth.

"What does it taste like?" Anna asked.

"What's the flavor?" Friede begged.

"Is it good?" the children whispered to him. Their eyes glued to his face.

"Mmmmmmm," was all he could say. Mendel, having never had a butterscotch before, really had no words to describe the buttery creamy sweet. That, however, was all they needed. One by one the children reached into the paper bag, randomly selected a treat, and popped it into their mouths. They stood transfixed and then vainly tried to explain the flavors to each other.

While the children were thusly engaged, Dr. Heard drove into the clearing and hitched his horse to one of the houses. Ruchel, having heard the commotion, came down to see. She smiled brightly when she realized it was the doctor. Dr. Heard was surprised and pleased to receive a hug from the matriarch of the community.

"Tank you, tank you," she repeated enthusiastically and dragged him into the house before he had time to grab his bag or share the supplies he had brought.

The last few patients were on the floor. The doctor went over to check on them. He did so hesitantly because he knew that if the quinine had not worked by now, it would not. It was as he feared. One of the men had lapsed into a coma and another had a seizure as the doctor checked his pulse.

"Let me get my bag," he mumbled as he stood up and left the room. With a heavy heart he grabbed his doctor's bag and a crate of supplies. He lugged the crate upstairs and dropped it on the table. "Ruchel, come here. I've supplies." When Ruchel came over, he pulled sacks of corn meal, sugar, and coffee out of the crate. Then out came another tin of the blackberry paste and another tin of quinine. "This is more corn meal, sugar, and coffee in my wagon."

Ruchel took his hand with tears in her eyes. "No pay," she said in broken English.

"Oh, no problem," Dr. Heard said reassuringly. "You can pay me for the paste and quinine when you can, and the Adler family sent the supplies. They said to tell you '*tzeddakah*[16] is a *mitzvah*[17].'"

Moyshe, having heard the news the doctor was in the clearing, had left the river where he had gone to check the water levels and hurried back. He too was worried about the few remaining sick men.

The responsibility of having convinced all these people to follow him weighed heavily on his conscience.

"Doktor, Doktor, our friend," he said excitedly as they shook hands. "Tank, tank, for the medicine."

"Absolutely," the doctor replied. "I am here to help, but these few men. I don't know. I have seen this before and..."

He was interrupted by Ruchel's curt, "Doktor!" and then her sobbing.

Heard dashed over to where Ruchel sat on the floor gently holding the hand of the man who had been in a coma. She looked up him sadly, tears rolling down her face. He dropped to his knees on the other side of the man and took his wrist. There was no pulse. The doctor took a deep breath; this was a part of his job he had never found a way to accept. Reaching across the body, the doctor put his hand on Ruchel's as a sign of comfort. Moyshe came over and put his hand on Ruchel's shoulder. The three stayed in this tableau for a few minutes and then the mood was broken. The man next to him had another seizure.

The doctor switched modes from comforter to lifesaver. He grabbed a wooden spoon from the table and forced it into the man's mouth to keep the patient from biting his tongue and breaking his teeth. The man was forced to bite down on the handle of the spoon. There was nothing else the doctor could do. When the man relaxed, the doctor removed the spoon and took his stethoscope out of his bag. Gently, Heard pulled back the blanket and opened the man's shirt. He watched the chest rise and fall slowly and shallowly until it stopped. The doctor was not surprised, but he was sad. Putting the earpieces in his ears, the doctor put the funnel of his scope on the man's chest. Then, with a heavier heart, he looked up at Ruchel and Moyshe and shook his head "no." Ruchel turned away and hid her face in Moyshe's thigh sobbing. Heard pulled the blankets over the faces of the two dead man and moved to help the other five men who were living. While they were weak, they were clearly on the mend. He mixed a lot of sugar in the pot of coffee and filled five mugs half full. Ruchel and Moyshe immediately understood his actions and came to help. Gently, they spoon fed the men the sugary coffee.

As they were finishing, Yosef followed by his brother Zundel, dashed in. "Doktor," he gleefully shouted.

"I am so glad to see you so well," the doctor grinned.

"Medicine is good."

"The quinine surely does the job," and the two men warmly shook hands.

Zundel stopped short and pulled his twin's sleeve. "What happened?" he asked in Russian.

"They have died," Ruchel answered sadly.

Zundel went over to uncover their faces and let out a cry.

"I'm so sorry," the doctor said. "The quinine does work all the time, but medicine can only do so much. And you are eating so little." And he patted Zundel on the back.

Moyshe took a deep breath, "Where do we bury them? We don't have a graveyard."

Dr. Heard didn't understand the Russian, but he understood the sentiment. "Zundel, you and your brother can put these men," and he pointed to the two who had just died, "in my wagon" and he pointed out the window. "The Adler family said they would take care of your dead. There are also bags of supplies in the wagon that I brought for you."

Yosef couldn't speak, but he nodded his assent. He looked at Zundel and cocked an eyebrow. Zundel nodded. They rolled each man in his blanket, and each took an end of one of the blanket rolls and awkwardly carried him across the room and down the stairs. Dr. Heard washed his hands with some of the soap he had brought and methodically folded his stethoscope and put it back in his bag.

Moyshe approached him, "Tank Adlers. How we pay?"

"I've no idea. When you come to Newport, I will introduce you and you can figure it out. Until then, just know that the Adlers are very generous people."

When Yosef and Zundel returned, each with a crate of supplies, Dr. Heard took his coat and bag. As they carried the second body down the stairs, the doctor followed. The twins loaded the corpses into the wagon and the doctor circled the clearing. He stopped everyone he saw and felt their forehead and checked their pulse. He was quite pleased with everyone he met.

Men started to return for the evening. They were hot and sweaty and had their shirts flung over their shoulders as padding for the tools. They stumbled exhausted through the clearing and dumped their saws and axes in a pile and headed towards the river to wash.

"Zundel," Dr. Heard called out, "Do you all work without your shirts?"

"*Da*, it is hot," John answered.

"You must not. Tell the men that is dangerous. Quinine makes you sensitive to the sun. You will burn."

Zundel looked at him quizzically and shook his head with confusion. However, as the men drew near, he saw that their skin was bright red. "*Da*, I will tell," he agreed.

Ruchel, having come down out of one house, searched for Dr. Heard. "Doktor," she called. "Doktor! Some supper."

The doctor turned to Ruchel. He knew that he could not refuse this simple meal of corncake and coffee. These people had no other way of paying him. Everyone knew that he was eating the food he had brought but Heard was certainly not going to point that out.

With a gracious smile, he said, "Thank you" and took the plate and mug that were proffered.

When he finished, he returned the mug and plate to Ruchel, who had watched him eat the meal. He smiled and nodded his appreciation, tousled Hirsch's hair, and unhitched the horse. As he turned the wagon around, the children ran to him begging for more candy.

"No more today, children," he laughed. "Moyshe, I will return in a few weeks to check on all of you." Then the doctor climbed into his wagon and headed back to town with the two corpses.

17

The Store

"Hannah, Anna, come here," called Ruchel.

Hannah and Anna came quickly. They knew better than to disobey their mother.

"Girls, I want you to go to Everly's store and get some corn meal. Ask if we can pay later."

"Yes, Mamma," Anna answered.

"Can I go?", Gittel asked.

"No, little girl," replied Ruchel. "You need to stay here and help me by minding Saul."

Gittel gave a soft sigh and turned back to washing the dishes.

"Off you go girls! Don't dawdle," commanded their mother.

The girls dashed off. They had walked to the store numerous times before with their mother and father and sometimes with the other children. This was the first time they would go alone together. Holding hands, they skipped towards the path that would lead them towards the crossroads where Everly's store was. No one in the commune was exactly sure of the name of the man who ran the store. Every time someone had asked, it sounded like Everly.

The girls sang songs as they walked the path. Sometimes they tried to imitate the birds' songs. This caused them to laugh hysterically as neither was any good at this. They admired the flowers. On occasion, they stopped to pick some and then as they walked, they tried to twist them into crowns. Then they saw a family of rabbits.

Hannah suggested, "We should go and visit the rabbits."

"Don't be silly," Anna retorted. "Mamma sent us to the store. We don't have time to stop."

"Just a few moments," begged her sister. "They are adorable!"

"No! We have a job to do. Besides, I am the older sister, and you have to do as I say."

"You're not Mamma! And you're not that much older than me," snapped Hannah. "Just a few minutes to see the babies." And off she crept to see the nest of baby rabbits under the big pine tree.

"That's it. I'm going on without you," Anna shouted and stomped onward. Only a few paces did she take when something glistened at her feet among the leaves. Anna bent over and reached for it. She screamed, "Eeeeeeeeeeeeeeeeee!" and dashed back to her sister shaking.

"Anna? Anna!," Hannah shook her sister, "What's the matter?"

"A sn...a sn...a snake," squealed Anna.

"A snake?" screamed Hannah. Hannah grabbed Anna's hand and the two started running home. They sobbed the entire way.

As they entered the clearing the little children waved. Gittel looked up curiously, "What's the matter?" she called out.

Her sisters didn't acknowledge her. They ran to their house and up the stairs. At no point did they unclasp their hand or stop sobbing. They only stopped when their mother opened her arms and they collided with her.

"Little chickens," she said soothingly, "whatever is the matter?"

They were too hysterical to answer. Shaking and sobbing, they nestled in even closer to their mother, almost knocking her over.

"Come, let us sit down," She suggested gently. And the three stumbled over to the mattress on the floor in the corner of the room. In unison, they dropped onto it. "Hush, babies, hush," she cooed trying to get them to relax.

By now Gittel and the little ones had made it upstairs.

"Mamma?" Gittel asked with concern.

Ruchel looked up at her and shook her head "no." Then she gave her third daughter a stern look and flicked her right hand from behind Anna's back. Gittel gathered up the little ones yet again and went back outside.

For quite a while, Ruchel sat on the mattress with a daughter wrapped in each arm. She hummed lullabies and rocked them, just as she had when they were babies. It took some time, but the girls finally stopped sobbing.

"Now, little chickens, tell your mamma what upset you so," Ruchel whispered.

"We...we...we were walking straight to the st...st...store," stuttered Anna.

"Yes, straight," repeated Hannah.

"I am quite sure," agreed their mother, although she was positive that wasn't exactly true.

"And I saw something pretty in the leaves on the path," Anna whispered slowly gaining control.

"I didn't see it," Hannah added in a panicked voice.

Ruchel continued to hold them close and stroke their hair.

Anna continued, "I went to pick it up." Her voice started to shake.

"Sh...shhhhhhh," her mother whispered, still rocking.

"It...it...it was a sn...a sn...snake," and Anna began to cry again.

Hannah let out a sympathetic scream.

"It's ok. It's ok," Ruchel cooed. "There are no bad snakes here. Remember, I said you must be very careful in this new place. There are creatures, like snakes, we know nothing about."

"I know. I know," Anna said as she started to cry again.

"Shhhhhhhhh," Ruchel whispered as she lay them each down. "Nothing will harm you here. Go to sleep." And she covered the girls with a blanket. The two girls hugged each other close as they relaxed into sleep.

18

The Boys' Failure

The summer days seemed endless. As May became June and June edged towards July, the heat became worse, and the rainstorms ensured that the mosquitos flourished, and it was impossible to float the logs to Newport. Moyshe became more and more convinced that this experiment was untenable, but he did not believe that they had any choice other than to stick it out.

Adding quinine to the morning coffee became a habit for Ruchel. Ruchel became adept at stretching the little food they had until one day there was nothing left. By this time, she had very little energy left for self-pity. Instead, every time some event slapped her down, she immediately tried to problem solve. They had to have food and food cost money. There was nothing to do but find any pennies they had left. So, she went to every person in the commune and begged any penny anyone had left.

"Mordechai," she called out.

He turned and walked towards her, "I'm about to leave for the woods."

"I know," she responded. "I was hoping that you would go to Ellery's and ask him if we could borrow his horse and wagon because we a have a big order."

"Me?" he asked.

"You have a good relationship with him. If he will let us, you are the one who will convince him."

"Then I will try," he answered and headed off with his axe and saw over one shoulder. The rest of the men were leaving or had left to find trees to fell.

Ruchel sought out Anna and Sheyndel, "We have nothing left. What should we get with this money?" And she held out a bowl filled with the pennies and nickels everyone had donated.

Penny

Anna blurted out, "Flour!"

"And whey and kerosene," added Sheyndel.

"Of course, corn meal," Ruchel stated.

"Will there be any coffee?" asked Anna.

"Well, we need that too," was Ruchel's despondent answer.

"And who's going to the store?" Sheyndel asked.

Hirsch was standing nearby, "I can go."

Abraham called out, "What about me? I can do it!"

"You're not going without me," his brother yelled dropping out of a tree.

Mendel followed him more cautiously climbing down, "If they go, I go."

The mothers looked at each other.

"Who knows how to drive a horse and wagon?" asked Sheyndel.

Nickel

"I do," they all answered.

"Well," began Ruchel, "I guess you all can go."

Shouts of "hurrah" were heard as the boys jumped up and down.

"Hush," commented Ruchel, "I need to give you our list. This is terribly important, boys. We are going to give you the last of our money."

Hirsh put on his stern face, "Yes, ma'am. I'll be in charge. You can trust me."

The other boys started crying out that "that's unfair" and "what makes him special?"

"Boys, figure it out," Sheyndel commanded. "We need these supplies, and we are sending you."

Anna took the kerchief off her hair and held it open towards Ruchel. Ruchel carefully poured the coins into the kerchief. While Anna held the mass of coins in her two hands, Ruchel carefully tied the kerchief into a bundle.

Sheyndel turned to the boys, "Here is our list. Repeat after me." The boys gathered round her, each trying to impress her so that they would be put in charge. "Flour."

"Flour," they all said in unison.

"Coffee," she announced.

"Coffee," they repeated.

"Kerosene," she stated.

"Kerosene," they shouted.

"Whey," Sheyndel said,

"Whey," they responded curiously.

"Corn meal."

"Corn meal."

"Good, now repeat the list," she requested.

Like soldiers, they stood in a row and called out in union, "Flour. Coffee. Kerosene. Whey. Corn meal."

Anna realized what the boys were about. "Good men," she announced. "As Hirsch is the eldest, he can carry the money." A groan rose up among the others. "But your job is to protect him from ruffians. Now, off you go. We can't have supper until you get home."

With a whoop and much hollering, the boys dashed off towards Ellery's store. Hirsch held the kerchief of money in his arm much like a football player carries a football.

With that taken care of the women got back to work. Anna and Mrs. Goldstein had gathered the laundry.

"I'm not sure how we are going to clean these without soap," Mrs. Goldstein commented despondently. Everyone had grown to expect the most negative of comments from Mrs. Goldstein. It grated on them.

Anna, ever cheerful, did her best to be positive, "We will do the best we can with a washboard and clean water." She picked up the basket of laundry and headed off to the river.

Sheyndel went off into the woods to look for edibles that could supplement their diet. Dandelion greens were not a favorite but helped with variety. Wild onion grass added a welcome addition to the corn-cakes and with the vast amounts of rain, she was hoping to find some edible mushrooms.

Ruchel stayed in the clearing picking up after the men. Some had gotten into the habit of leaving mugs and plates by their bedrolls. The community had also learned that hanging the blankets, rather than leaving them on the ground, kept the blankets drier and the snakes and crawlies out of them.

When the women had finished their chores, they gathered in the shade. Ruchel and Anna rocked their little ones and they all sat enjoying the respite.

"I hear the wagon," Mrs. Goldstein mumbled in the drowsy state.

"So do I," chirped Anna, who was always excited to see her children.

Ruchel cocked her head, "They aren't being noisy. That's odd."

"You're right," agreed Sheyndel. "I'd have expected singing or cheering considering their mood when they left."

The women slowly rose to their feet. There was no hurry as the wagon was a bit of a way off, plus Anna and Ruchel had no desire to awaken their little ones. The girls, who had been in one of the houses mending heard the wagon and came down the stairs to greet their brothers. They too were whispering among themselves about the quiet.

When the wagon entered the clearing, it was obvious something was wrong. The boys let up a wail as if someone had died. Hirsch, who was driving the wagon, remained entirely static. So still was he that Anna at first thought him dead, until he pulled the reins and let out a loud, "Whoa!" For a moment, even the birds were silent. No one moved.

Then Mendel, who could never keep a secret or follow directions, let out a cry, "Oh Mamma!"

Suddenly, the wagon was full of weepy little boys. They had left as little men and returned as children. However, they were too afraid to come off the wagon and face their mothers. They sat in the wagon and on the wagon seat and cried.

Finally, Sheyndel reached up to help Mendel down, "Tell me, my son, what has happened? It cannot be that terrible."

Mendel reached down for his mother and cried out, "Don't hate us! I didn't do it."

That broke the damn. All the boys, but Hirsch, jumped off the wagon and began talking at once. It was impossible to tell what they were saying through the cacophony of the multiple voices and crying.

Ruchel pushed through the boys and put a hand on the wagon seat. She looked up at the silent Hirsch and commanded, "Tell the story."

The boys became silent except for some sniffles. They stood with their heads hung down and their legs shaking.

Hirsch could not look at Ruchel or his mother or any of the women. He stared straight ahead and began in a barely audible monotone, "We got to Everly's fine. He said Papa had come already and we could borrow the wagon, but it has to be returned today. We…we…we gave him our order and I put the money on the counter. I didn't let any of the boys have anything – no sweets, no toys. Everly counted the money and we had just enough. We carried the sacks to the wagon, and he taught us how to 'hitch', yes that's the word, 'hitch' the horse. I promised three times to bring back the wagon today and everyone climbed in."

"Well done," complimented Anna, wiping tears from Mendel's face with her thumbs.

"And then…then…it happened," and here Hirsch broke down. He couldn't go on.

The rest of the boys took over the story, but all the women heard was "fight" and "sorry."

Sheyndel shouted, "Halt! I don't understand this garble. Hirsch, take a deep breath and start again."

He looked at her frightened and then looked down at his boots and began again, "I don't know exactly what happened. I should have been more aware, but I was trying to control the horse. It isn't as easy as it looks, you know. The next thing I knew there was a fight back there." He pointed in the back with his thumb over his shoulder.

"I didn't start it," interjected Mendel defensively.

"I'm sure you didn't," his mother responded gently.

"I don't know what it was about," Hirsch repeated.

"It doesn't matter," his mother answered softly.

"And then...and then...," Hirsch stuttered.

Isaac jumped in here, "None of us meant it to happen."

"Good heavens," Mrs. Goldstein blurted out in frustration, "Would someone please tell us what this terrible thing is that happened?"

Again, a terrible silence. Only the woodpecker could be heard tapping out a desperate rhythm. The boys looked at each other guiltily, daring someone else to say it.

Hirsch took a deep breath and spat out, "The kerosene was knocked over."

The boys all flinched as if someone had hit them.

The girls all stepped back unsure what would happen.

The women looked at each other in horror and then ran to the wagon. They hoped beyond hope that this was some joke. It was not. The tin can of kerosene, two gallons of kerosene, was tipped over and the lid was nowhere to be seen. The women began to wail as if they were at a funeral.

"Our kerosene," cried Ruchel.

"All of our kerosene," whimpered Sheyndel.

Mrs. Goldstein, who could be counted on to make everyone feel as miserable as she was, remarked, "I knew we shouldn't have sent the boys."

The boys didn't move. Hirsch remained immobile on the wagon seat.

The girls rushed over, climbing on the wagon wheels for a better view.

"Where did all the kerosene go?" asked Gittel bewildered.

"Yes, where?" asked Friede. "It isn't anywhere to be seen."

Ruchel touched the sack of flour next to the can that had held the kerosene. She lifted her fingers to her nose. Then she looked up at the sky, her eyes glistening with tears.

When she had recovered herself, she said out loud to nobody and to everybody, "The flour has soaked up all the kerosene."

The other women hissed as they drew in air. The girls backed away from the wagon, unwilling to be part of what came next, but too curious to leave.

Mrs. Goldstein finally reached out and grabbed a boy. It happened to be Isaac. She beat him on the head with her first.

"You stupid, stupid boy," she cried over and over until Ruchel grabbed her arms and Anna took her son away.

Sheyndel took action, "Boys, all the sacks must be taken inside. Then you are to scrub this wagon, so it does not smell of kerosene. When that is done, Hirsch, you shall take the wagon back and thank Mr. Everly. And the rest of you will go to the river and wash yourselves and the clothes you are wearing."

The boys looked at each other in shock. They had really expected a beating. This seemed too good to be true. In silence they unloaded the wagon, washed it, watered the horse, and sent Hirsch back to the store. Then the subdued Mendel, Abraham, and Isaac went to the river.

While all this was going on, the women gather around the damaged bag of flour.

Sheyndel, looking despondent, started the discussion, "What shall we do with this bag of flour?"

"We have to use it," Ruchel sighed.

"We cannot," retorted Mrs. Goldstein. "It has kerosene in it."

"What else is there to eat?" asked Ruchel pragmatically. "We have only what the boys brought back today to feed us until the lumber can be gotten to Newport."

"That is true," agreed Anna. "There is no more money to buy food and we are stretching this as far as we can."

The decision was made without any real discussion. There was no choice. They had to eat it.

After a few days, the women all agreed that they really couldn't taste the kerosene at all.

19

The Cabin

Ruchel had made it quite clear that she was not pleased with the living conditions in Arkansas. Along with everyone else, the heat, mosquitos, and snakes, the housing was unsanitary and crowded. Moyshe did not like the housing either.

Unbeknownst to Ruchel, Moyshe convinced Everly to let him build a house near the communal clearing. There he got two members of the commune to help him start the house. Later, when the Herder children went to school, they called that house the Lincoln cabin because it was built with those same logs in that same style. Once it was started, the men went off to work on the cutting of the railroad ties. When the men left, Moyshe would find Anna, Hannah, or Gittel to help him. They would hand him tools and look for lost nails in the ground. They would fetch him water to drink and keep his spirits up with their endless questions about the house and the world around them. It did not take long for Moyshe to finish the house, including the roof.

Then Moyshe began the furniture. He didn't plan on anything fancy. He wasn't a carpenter. He really had not built anything before coming to the New World. First, he constructed a simple table that he attached to one side of the room. By attaching it to the wall, he only had to make one pair of legs and he would ensure the table did not wobble. Then he made a pair of benches for the table. These he attached to the earthen floor. Near the door, he attached a shelf, made like the table with only two legs. Finally, he made two beds. They were very much like the table only lower to the ground.

"Who are the beds for?" asked Hannah as she helped him.

"One, my little kitten," he answered cheerfully as he sawed, "is for you girls and one is for Mamma and me."

"What about Saul?"

"Ah, Saul will sleep with us, until he is ready for his own bed and then I will build it."

"Oh," she answered amazed at her father's skills.

When it was finished, Moyshe made a show of bringing Ruchel to her new home.

He collected her at the communal house, "My fair lady, would you come for walk in the woods with me to see your new cottage?"

Ruchel could not help but play along, "My dear sir, I am most honored to come with you for a stroll." And she tightened her *babushka* and looped her arm into his.

He walked her through the woods a short way to a fresh clearing with a little cabin in it. It wasn't more than a room, but Ruchel was so thrilled she started to cry. After going inside and examining everything, Ruchel kissed her husband and gave him a long, heartfelt hug.

"I shall get the children and we will move in immediately! Thank you, my wonderful husband. Now, we can have some privacy."

The two returned to the main group more light-hearted than they had been for many months. Ruchel called the children, and they gathered their few items of clothing, rolled up their bedding, and collected their dishes and *samovar*. Then, like a mother duck leading her ducklings, Ruchel marched her children to their new home.

It did not take long for her to organize the cabin. She hung their few spare items of clothes on the nails Moyshe had hammered in the wall by the door. The girls unrolled the bedding in the two bed frames their father had built. The dishes went on the little shelf over the table.

Only when the samovar was unwrapped and placed on the shelf by the door did Ruchel believe her unpacking all was done.

Ruchel went outside and found a suitable place for a firepit. Once she located it, she sent Hannah back to the commune for a shovel. Ruchel and the rest of the children scavenged for firewood and had started a good pile under one of the eaves by the time Hannah returned.

That evening when Moyshe came home to his cabin, he found the children playing hide-and-seek and his wife making corn cakes over their own fire. This little vignette of domesticity warmed his heart and renewed his hope that they would survive.

All seemed safe and well for a while for the Herder family. After many months, Moyshe was finally sleeping inside away from the morning dew and night-time storms. Ruchel no longer awoke at night concerned about where her husband was. When she opened her eyes, her husband's snoring put her back to sleep.

And then a vicious thunderstorm came across the woods one night.

"Papa!" called out Saul as a thunderclap shook the house.

Moyshe reached for the boy and tucked him between himself and Ruchel, "It is just a rainstorm, son. We are safe and dry in our house." Ruchel rolled over and sleepily hummed a lullaby into Saul's ear.

Then Anna called out, "Papa, someone has peed in the bed."

"Not me!" called out Hannah.

"Nor me!" cried Gittel.

With the next thunderclap came a bright light and Moyshe realized what had happened. He had not sealed the roof well. In an effort to not wake his wife, he quietly rolled out of bed and walked the few paces to the girls' bed.

"Hush now," he quietly reassured them. "It is no one's fault but nature's. Take your bedding under the table. It should protect you from the rain."

As quickly as they could, the three girls took their mattress and blanket and dragged them under the table. As they settled in, Moyshe handed them a sleeping Saul. The three made room for their little brother and tried to sleep as the cabin rattled around them and the dripping in their home turned into a flow of water.

When the family awoke, everyone was wet and everything was soaked.

Anna whispered in Hannah's ear, "I'm surprised we didn't float away like Noah's ark."

Hannah giggled.

Ruchel was frustrated and angry at their situation and her husband for not being a better carpenter. Even if she had heard the joke she would not have been amused.

"Up children," she demanded. "There will be no breakfast until we get everything outside to dry. You can roll out from under the table and get started."

Dutifully, the children complied. One by one, they rolled out from under the table and stood in the mud that had been their floor. Then they just looked at each other. It was difficult to even think of where to begin.

"Eeeeeeeeeeeeeee!" screamed their mother.

The four children miraculously appeared next to their distraught mother. Ruchel stood still, her mouth open, holding up a sopping pillow with one hand. The other pointed at a big black snake as it slithered down one of the bed legs and out the door.

"Oh my," Ruchel sobbed as she dropped the pillow and then herself onto the bed. She grabbed her four children into a big hug and continued sobbing. "Oh my, we could have died. Did you see that horrible snake? My poor little chicks." On and on she continued until Saul squirmed out of her grasp.

Black Snake
Fredericksburg Tour, Black Snake. United States Fredericksburg Virginia Fredericksburg County, 1920. Library of Congress, www.loc.gov/item/2016828088/.

Then the spell was broken, and the family began dragging everything outside to dry out.

When Moyshe returned in the late afternoon, Ruchel was prepared to berate him. By that time, the black snake had become the size of a boa constrictor and had spoken like the snake in the Garden of Eden.

20

The Farm

As the men were rising from their afternoon naps, Hirsch came bounding into the clearing.

"Someone is coming!" he shouted.

The men pulled on their boots and rolled up their bedding. Visitors were a rarity, and everyone wanted to present themselves as best they could.

"Who is it?" someone called out.

"I think it is the neighbor farmer," responded Hirsch.

The men looked at each other curiously. Ruchel had heard the dialogue and came down with a clean mug so she could offer the guest at least some coffee.

Hirsch was correct. About twenty minutes later in wandered their neighbor who lived three miles south. Moyshe and Yosef approached him. Moyshe as the *defacto* leader of the community and Zundel because his English was perhaps the best of the group. The men shook hands.

"I have a problem and hope you can help me," the farmer began.

Moyshe raised an eyebrow. "What do we have that someone would want?" he wondered.

"Please," he responded.

"I am short-handed. I heard you have some men who might like some work. I'd be willing to pay."

Yosef immediately became interested, "How much? What kind of work?"

"Well," began the farmer, "I could use about forty men to weed my tobacco fields. Not only will I pay one dollar seventy per day for each person and I'll house and feed them for the time it should take to do this work."

Now both Moyshe and Yosef were intrigued. Yosef thought of the meals he and his brother could get and the money. Moyshe was interested in how much further their rations could go if they didn't have to feed twenty people for two weeks.

"When to start?" Moyshe asked in his basic English.

"Tomorrow would be perfect," The farmer answered. When Ruchel approached him with a mug of coffee, he waved her away. "No thank you. I really must go. There is much to do at my farm. Can you send men?"

"Sure. Sure," Moyshe agreed. "Tomorrow."

The men all shook hands and the farmer walked purposely back into the woods. Moyshe and Zundel stood where they had been left until he disappeared into the trees. Then they turned to each other and hugged.

Tears ran down Moyshe face, "We are saved."

The various members of *Am Olam* gathered round Moyshe and Yosef asking what the story was.

"Gentlemen, we have an offer that could save us," Moyshe announced.

A joyful "whoop" went through the crowd.

"I need forty volunteers," he continued, "who will spend time at our neighbor's farm. He has promised room and food for the duration of work along with cash. One dollar and seventy-five cents per day of labor per person."

Another louder "whoop" went through the men. They started to push forward. Each wanted the honor and pleasure of going to a productive farm. Moyshe looked around him at the eager faces. He pondered the choices and settled on twenty men, including Menaker and Spies, who had some farming experience, even though the request had been for forty. He did not want to send men he didn't think could do the work. Then all the men went off to do their evening lumber work.

At first light, the twenty men rose as always, with all the other men. Like everyone else they put on their boots, but they rolled up their blankets rather than hang them in the trees to dry. Like everyone else, they waited for a corncake for breakfast and a mug of water. Unlike the others who went in pairs into the woods, these men gathered at the edge of the clearing with their bedrolls under an arm and then walked off into the woods taking the same path that the farmer had. It was early and they were a little anxious and so they walked in silence.

In about an hour, they arrived at the farm. In the distance, they saw the farmer and waved. When he didn't respond, they let a single "howdy" that was carried across the field by a gust of wind. The farmer turned and waved. They waved back and headed towards him as he moved towards them. When they met the farmer shook some hands and took them to the barn to leave their bedrolls.

"Now, we begin," he announced. "Bring your water and gloves and let's get to work."

Willingly the twenty men followed him out into the tobacco field though they had no gloves. There he showed them what was weed and what was tobacco. In relative silence, save for the buzzing of flies and mosquitos and swishing of the leaves, the first hour passed. The farmer watched as he worked and saw that these men, while willing, were really unfit for this job. They spent more time wiping their foreheads and stretching their backs than weeding. After another hour, almost all the men were exhausted.

Working on a Tobacco Farm
Lange, Dorothea, photographer. Tobacco field, early morning, where white sharecropper and wage laborer are priming tobacco. Shoofly, Granville County, North Carolina. 1939. July. Library of Congress, www.loc.gov/item/2017772409/.

"Stop," called out the farmer. "This is not working. You cannot do this. Go home."

As hungry and desperate as these men were, they were thrilled to be let go. This was much harder than they had thought it would be. The farmer walked over to Menaker and Spies and said to them quietly, "Stay if you like. You seem able to do this work."

Menaker turned to Spies and said in Russian, "Do we have a choice? Who else will make the money?"

His companion replied, "Where else will we get supper?"

Thus, the two stayed. They did the backbreaking work for ten days with the farmer and his wife, when she was done with her most basic chores. Each day the farmer's wife gave them a hearty breakfast and each evening they ate a good supper.

When the work was finished, the famer handed them $35.

"No," Spies insisted, "food, please."

"Yes, please, food," Menacker repeated.

After his initial visit nearly two weeks before, the farmer understood their desperation. "Absolutely," he agreed. Together with the two men, he loaded the wagon with whatever foodstuffs he could part with: flour, bacon, corn meal, coffee, sugar, and beans. Then hitched the horses to it.

"Bring it back tomorrow, empty," he said quietly. "Thank you very much for your help." And he and his wife waved goodbye as Spies and Menaker disappeared into the woods.

The ride back was much quicker than the walk out had been. When they arrived with a wagon of food, a holler was cheered, and everyone came running. The two men made sure everyone got a fair portion of their supplies.

Moyshe hugged each of them in thanks and called them saviors.

21

The Tree

The rains came again, and they were torrential. Over and over again, the rain fell from the sky. Everything was wet. There was no way to dry out the bedding, the clothes, or even the food.

When they could not imagine the weather getting any worse, the most violent storm yet appeared. The thunder was deafening and the rain piercing.

Abe looked at his boys through a wall of rain. They looked like drowning rats. The three jumped as another crack of lightening shook everything.

"We should go inside," he shouted.

"What, Papa?" Yosef asked, deafened by the rain and thunder.

Abe stood up and motioned for his boys to follow. They stood up and followed him. All the men did so. The men struggled through the muck and rain into the building. The women put the children on the table and the adults crowded in together. They sat with their knees bent up to their chests. There was no way to walk around. There they sat, huddled together, wet and dry, waiting for the storm to pass.

Suddenly, the room lit up and at almost the same moment, the loudest clap of thunder was heard. The women and children let up a wail.

Then, much to everyone's horror, they heard a crack and in the lull of the storm, there was a creak.

Mordechai, who was sitting under the window getting wet, stood up and opened the shutter to see outside.

"Oy! *Ha shem*[18]!" he cried out.

"What? Tell us all!" called out various members of the crowd.

Mordechai slowly closed the shutter, turned around carefully to not trip over anyone, and held onto the wall. He swallowed hard and called out in a shaky voice to be heard over the storm, "The tr...tr...tree. It's gone."

Unable to believe his ears, Abe Goldstein yelled, "What tree?"

"The tree by the house," Mordechai responded.

The entire group sucked in their breath in horror. Moyshe began a prayer of thanks to God that everyone joined in with.

When the storm ended, one by one the group left the building. They stood together on the swampy ground staring at the pine that had fallen. It lay next to their house, so close that one could not pass between them.

Mordechai held Ruchel close, "*Baruch ha-shem,*[19]" he whispered.

"Amen," was her answer.

22

The Fever Returns

All summer, Dr. Heard would visit at irregular intervals. He was always welcomed. The children clambered around him waiting for a piece of the candy he always brought them.

Ruchel enjoyed his visits, as well. He brought her new supplies of quinine and checked in on the injured. Most of the injuries were splinters and twisted ankles, things Ruchel could handle quite well. Sometimes there was someone with a relapse of malarial fever. This time after the fall of the tree was difficult.

When Dr. Heard arrived in the clearing, the children ran after him begging for their treats, which he gladly shared. Ruchel, however, magically showed up next to the doctor with a strained look on her face.

"Ruchel, whatever is the matter?" he inquired with concern.

"The malaria," she answered. "This time different."

Dr. Heard looked at her curiously and grabbed his bag and followed her. She had learned from him and set up a quarantine as best she could. There were the forty worst cases of malaria fever in the camp. The doctor was immediately worried.

"You gave them all quinine," he asked curtly.

"*Da*," she answered.

"I'm so sorry," he responded gently. "I know you have."

"Not good," she stated flatly.

He looked around the clearing. Here lay forty men shivering in the hot summer sun. Some were vomiting.

"Have any others been sick?" he inquired.

Ruchel looked at him with sad tired eyes, "All. Hot heads and then good, this. Hot heads and then good, this......," her voice trailed off.

The doctor knelt down next to one of the men. He opened the man's eye and saw that it was bloodshot as if he were drunk. The doctor's heart dropped. He opened the man's mouth and gently pulled out his tongue. It was fuzzy. Hesitantly, the doctor checked the man's pulse. It was unusually slow. Without commenting, he checked the next man and the next and found the same symptoms. He fell back into a sitting position.

Ruchel immediately knew something was wrong, "What Doktur?" she said hesitantly.

As he sat there, one and then another of the men vomited. He saw that it was black and now his diagnosis was assured.

"Yellow Jack," he mumbled under his breath. "Dang it!"

"Excuse?" asked Ruchel.

"This is yellow jack. At least that's what the locals call it. It is also called yellow fever. It is nasty. I bet everyone's had a bout, but these men are the worst," he responded sadly.

"*Frau* Goodman," added Ruchel.

"What? Oh no…the baby?" the doctor asked in a panic as he stood up.

Ruchel looked at the doctor desperately and then led him to a secluded spot under the trees. Anna lay there fevered, her eyes unseeing. Heard sat next to her and pulled back the covers. There was the baby Sheyndel in the same state, too tired to cry. He checked both their pulses. One was far too fast and the other far too slow. He opened her mouth gently to see her tongue. Anna's tongue was swollen and had a white coating on its surface.

He heaved a great sigh and turned to Ruchel with tears in his eyes, "I don't think she will make it and the baby certainly won't. Where is her husband?" And he stood after he replaced the blanket.

Ruchel's eyes flowed with tears of sadness and exhaustion. There were so few women in the commune, she knew Anna would be sorely missed by Sheyndel and herself. Quietly she led the doctor back to the men and to Hirsch Goodman.

"Good," declared the doctor after an examination. "He and many others can be saved."

One of the men began to hiccup terribly.

"Quick," commanded Heard, "put a pinch of sugar on his tongue." And he ran off to his horse for various medicines. Then he called to the children for a pot of hot water and asked some of healthy men to help.

"No worries, you've had it and won't get it again," he reassured them.

"First get them undressed if you can and clean up their mess. Some will have diarrhea and others will have vomited."

Some of the men whose English was not good looked at him curiously, so he mimed vomiting and squatting. They nodded.

"Let me know their symptoms," he called out as the men carefully cut their comrades out of their clothes. "Ruchel," he called her over. As he mixed two soup spoons of castor oil and added 15 drops of turpentine, he told her, "This mixture needs to be fed to every man who has had no bowel movement. I'll take care of the rest."

She grabbed the bowl, spoon, and bottle of turpentine. "Two of these" and she shook the spoon "and ten and five of this" and she held out the bottle.

"Yes," the doctor replied, pleased.

Off she trotted following her comrades who told her when someone was clean.

Then the doctor called for more water. This time from the river where it would be cool. As he proceeded through the men checking their symptoms giving every one of them a dose of quinine. For the men who were hot and dry, he called someone to wipe them with the cool river water. If their tongue was red and cracked, he administered an emulsion of turpentine.

A great cry arose when one of the patients began twitching. By the time the doctor got to him, the man had died. Carefully, Heard covered the man's face with his blanket and moved on. He stayed focused on saving as many as possible. There was no time to mourn.

After three long days of washing the men and administering turpentine tinctures and castor oil drinks and quinine, the yellow fever was over. Twenty weak men lay quietly under the cool trees being fed diluted coffee and sugar. On the other side of the clearing behind a blanket hanging from a tree branch was a make-shift morgue. There seventeen men, Anna Goodman, and her baby were wrapped in their blankets, which had to suffice for shrouds.

The three remining Goodman children sat around their father stone faced. They could not comprehend that their mother was dead, and their father was too weak to help them.

As tired as Dr. Heard was, he knew in this heat the bodies could not sit any longer.

He stumbled in exhaustion over to Moyshe, "Find a few strong men and load my wagon with the bodies. I will take them to be buried. I know Mr. Adler will make sure the burial is according to the custom of your people."

Moyshe nodded. He was too choked up to say anything. Taking Yosef and Zundel and another man, the four pulled back the blanket and sadly, slowly loaded the doctor's wagon.

The doctor took Moyshe's hand in a joyless handshake, "I'll be back in a few days to check on the patients." He couldn't bring himself to say survivors.

This time when he left there were no waving children. A cloud of melancholy covered the clearing.

23

The End

As promised, a few days later Dr. Heard returned. Hannah was the only child to greet him. She was amazingly sad.

"Papa needs to see you," she said pointing to the path to their home.

The doctor got down from the wagon and tied up his horse. He looked around and saw no one. Usually, the children were in the clearing playing or doing chores, but today only Hannah was there.

Cautiously, he strode down the path to the Herder cabin. There had been times when mourners had accused him of violence and accosted him. Moyshe was sitting out front on a stump sipping a cup of coffee. When he saw Dr. Heard, he rose, but did not wave. When the doctor arrived at the cabin, Moyshe offered him neither a seat nor a cup of coffee. Instead, without pleasantries he began the conversation.

"More dead. Please help."

Heard realized that something horrible had happened and quietly responded, "Anything." He had grown to appreciate these people who struggled so hard against all the odds.

"We pay someday," Moyshe continued.

Heard waved away that thought.

"Hirsch Goodman dead," Moyshe whispered, "Take Goodman three children to train. Telegram Jewish orphanage in New York City." With this last comment, Moyshe began to sob. He had encouraged all these people to follow his ideal of a new Jew and he had failed.

"Of course," Dr. Heard responded gently. "If this is what you think is best, then this is what I shall do. Don't worry about paying..." and here he stopped. Moyshe was not listening. Instead, he took Moyshe in a great bear hug.

When Moyshe was done sobbing, Dr. Heard released him. Together they walked back to the main clearing. The three orphaned siblings were already sitting on the wagon seat and two men were loading their father's body into the back. There were no good-byes; there was no waving.

Dr. Heard drove his wagon out of the clearing with Abraham, Friede, and Isaac. The *Am Olam* community, or what was left of them, stood by silently. The loss of these community members was hard. When Anna Goodman and her baby daughter had died from starvation and Yellow Fever, everyone felt the loss of their most positive member and littlest member. However, when her husband died from a broken heart and starvation and the children had to be sent back to New York City to an orphanage, the community broke. The realization that they were so poor, that their experiment was such a failure that they could not care for the children of their friends was crushing. Even worse was the knowledge that they could not afford to bury their dead or buy tickets for the orphans to travel. The Adler family covered all these expenses.

When the wagon became lost the people in the clearing, the *Am Olam* dispersed. The silence and sadness weighed heavily on the community. No one, not even the ever-verbal Mendel, broke the silence. Some of the men half-heartedly lifted their saws and axes and trudged off into the woods to attempt to cut trees. Those who remained took naps or pretended to. The children, unsure of what to do with themselves, went down to the river to talk amongst themselves and try to sort out what had happened. Their numbers were severely depleted.

Moyshe and Ruchel wandered hand-in-hand towards their little cabin. At first, they were silent, taking what little comfort they could from each other.

Then Ruchel broke the silence, "She was a sweet woman and a good friend."

"He was a solid member of our community," her husband responded.

"Have we failed them?" she asked, turning to him and making him stop.

Moyshe took a deep breath, "Failure means one doesn't do all they can. We have. Sending the three orphans back to New York is for the best. We cannot feed and clothe those children, forget educate them."

"True."

"And we cannot feed or clothe or educate our own children."

"Have we failed them?"

Moyshe looked up to the sky. If Ruchel had not known him so well, she would have thought him talking with God, but she knew he was thinking carefully about his answer.

Then he took her other hand and looked into her eyes, "We have not failed them, but I wonder if we could not do better. Look at the wonderful world they live in. Fresh air! The freedom to travel...."

"Fevers, death, and starvation," she retorted dryly.

"Dear, that is there, but this a large country," he said trying to lighten the mood.

"But we are here," and she dropped her eyes as tears began to fill her eyes. "I fear we have failed our children by staying here. We could provide better for them if we went elsewhere and that makes us failures."

Moyshe dropped her hands and used one hand to rub his forehead. He had pretended not to know this, but hearing his wife say the words had made them real. Coupled with the loss of one entire family to disease, starvation, and heartbreak, Moyshe realized at that moment this experiment had collapsed. It was not sustainable, and his ego was only hurting those he loved, those who depended upon him. His posture changed. His shoulders dropped and his feet began to drag.

Pileated Woodpecker
John James Audubon, "Pileated Woodpecker, Picus Pileatus," Birds of America, Bien Folio, 1860, Plate 257. Missouri History Museum, collections.mohistory.org/resource/886867.

Ever vigilant, Ruchel put her hand on her husband's shoulder in a comforting gesture. At first, he accepted it and then he rejected it, shrugging it off. They continued to stand still on the path, Moyshe staring into the woods without seeing and Ruchel staring at the back of Moyshe's head wishing there was something she could do to help them both. The air was still and in the distance could be heard the pounding of a woodpecker that echoed through the trees.

After an eternal five minutes, Moyshe turned and faced his wife. She saw something different in him. He took her hand and turned his sad eyes from hers to the path ahead. They returned to their silent march to their cabin. The only noise they made was the crunching of the leaves and twigs under their shoes.

When they arrived at the cabin, the couple released hands. Ruchel went to the edge of the clearing to find some kindling and logs for the fire she needed to build to make coffee. They had very little, and she had been saving it, but today seemed the day for the two to sit side-by-side while watching the sun set with a cup of coffee.

Moyshe, however, had a stronger purpose than he had had in a long while. When he entered the cabin, he went to the shelf opposite the bed. There he found a few sheets of paper, and envelope, his quill, and the pot of ink. He took these objects and shuffled to the table, leaving the door open to get the light and fresh air. He sat down and carefully stacked the sheets of paper in front of him. He opened the ink pot and dipped the pen in. Once more he stared off into space to compose himself and then he began the letter to end his failure to his children.

24

The Letter

20 August 1883

Dear Friends,

I write with a heavy heart. I beg of you to sacrifice your dreams and save us, your compatriots.

We were deceived about Arkansas, as we were about Louisiana. I have brought our people to a hellhole. We are all suffering from the ague and only because the doctor is a kind and generous man have we been able to get medication. We owe him much money. We have lost over 18 people to fevers and starvation, including Anna Goodman and her baby. Only because of the generosity of the local Jewish family have we been able to properly bury them. We only met this man, the patriarch, once, but he opened his heart to us. So much so that he personally paid for the burials. The Goodman children have been sent back to New York City to an orphanage because we cannot support them.

The heat here is unbearable during the summer months. We cannot work at all midday. The air is so wet, it was thick.

The land is not good for agriculture. The rains make it almost swampy. Thus, we have been reduced to felling trees. The term in English is 'lumberjacking.' It was not our intention, and the labor is terribly hard. The weather has worked against us here as well. To get the logs to market, we must use the river, but the rains make that impossible.

Yes, our lives have been a series of woes. We have lost all hope of making this community work and we have spent all our money. We are starving. We cannot stay here any longer and so I turn to you. Please, I beg you, send us money to leave. I ask you most humbly to hurry. Save us!

Most Humbly,
Moyshe Herder

25

Epilogue

Much of this story is true as are many of the experiences. I used the names these people were given by their parents, their Russian or Yiddish names. Other authors have used their Americanized names, and you will find those in this epilogue in parenthesis.

Am Olam

This organization began in Odessa, Russia in 1881. They were influenced by the desire of many Jews to be emancipated from the constraints put upon them by their fellow Jews and the Russians. One of the founders of the movement was Moyshe Herder. The *Am Olam* wanted to be agriculturalists to dispel the antisemitic notion that Jews were intellectuals and dependent upon others. Because of Russian laws, Jews were forbidden from owning land and so America was their only recourse.

While this community is referred to as the Newport, Arkansas community, they were not in or near the town. The best guess, because the location has been lost to history, is that the commune was 15 miles northeast of Newport, which put it halfway between Newport and Batesville. The events in Arkansas really did happen, though I did expand upon them. The *Am Olam* community in Arkansas tried desperately to thrive, but the poor land, weather, malaria, and yellow fever conspired against them. Between eighteen and twenty of them died. This community was the last to experience Yellow Fever in Arkansas.

Everyone left the Newport colony in 1883. The community went to St. Louis to a hospital and then most returned to New York City. Some left *Am Olam* and others stayed. The Herders, Woskobojnikoffs, and Mr. Goldstein, among others, founded a very successful commune in Vineland, New Jersey. It faded out of existence in the 1930s.

For more on the *Am Olam* experience in Arkansas:

"An Arkansas Colonization Episode," *Jewish Tribune*, 12 July 1929, reprinted in *Our Jewish Farmers and The Story of the Jewish Agricultural Society*, edited by Gabriel Davidson, L.B. Fischer Pub., 1943, 208-212.

Mara W. Cohen Ioannides. "Anti-Russian Sentiment among the Jews of St. Louis," *Gateway Magazine*, fall 2023, 6-15.

Ellen Eisenberg. *Jewish Agricultural Colonies in New Jersey, 1882-1920, (Utopianism and Communitarianism)*, Syracuse University Press, 1995.

Kate Herder. "Memories of Yesterday," *OzarksWatch: Documenting Jews of the Ozarks*, vol. 12, no. 1 & 2, 1999. 59-64.

Uri D. Herscher. *Jewish Agricultural Utopias in America, 1880-1910*, Wayne State University Press, 1981.

Abraha Menes, "The Am Oylam Movement," *American Jewish History*, vol. 1, ed. Jeffery S. Gurock, Routledge, 1988, 109-133.

Simon Adler

Simon Adler (1832-1904) arrived in Batesville, Arkansas (30 miles northeast of Newport) in 1850. He joined the Confederate Army, though he was against slavery. He opened the first bank in Batesville to help his fellow citizens better themselves, employed family and friends, and helped many of them to open their own businesses. He co-owned a business, with family members, in Newport and other communities in the area. Simon was one of the wealthiest people in the area and generous with his money.

Mr. Everly

Mr. Everly is mentioned in Kate Herder's memoir, but because she is unsure of his actual name, he is hard to locate.

Abe Goldstein

Abe Goldstein (1875-1941) was born in Russia and after living in Arkansas, he joined the Vineland, New Jersey commune. It is unclear if the Mrs. Goldstein mentioned by Kate Herder in the memoir is a relative of his or not. Here I made her his first wife. He married a woman 20-years his junior after moving to New Jersey and had three sons.

The Goodman family

There was a Goodman family on the *Bohemia* with the Herders. I assigned their names to our family: Hirsh (b. 1843), Anna (b. 1853), Abraham (b. 1874), Friede (b. 1874), Isaac (b. 1876) and Sheyndel (b. 1882). The *Bohemia* left Hamburg and landed at Crystal Island, New York 22 June 1882.

Dr. William Heard

Dr. William Heard (1853-1936) was one of the first physicians in Jackson County, Arkansas. He fought with the Confederates during the Civil War and graduated from the University of Louisville in 1869 as a physician.

Herder Family

Moyshe (Moses) Herder (1843-1911) was a founder of the *Am Olam Movement* in Odessa, Russia. As a private tutor, he spoke Russian, German, and Hebrew. He remained an intellectual his whole life and preferred thinking to physical labor. Around 1870, he married Ruchel (Rachel) (1847-?), who was four years younger than he. Together they had nine children, the first four born in Russia and are in this story: Anna (b. 1874), Hannah (b, 1876), Gittel (Katie) (b. 1877), and Saul (b. 1882). They did live in New York City for a short time before moving to Arkansas. After healing from their experience in Arkansas in St. Louis, they returned to New York City and eventually went to the *Am Olam* community in Vineland, New Jersey.

Solomon Menaker

Solomon Menaker was the leader of the Vilna *Am Olam* commune. He led the community in New York City and the failed Sicily Island, Louisiana commune. Menaker was hailed as the savior of the Newport colony because of his work at the tobacco farm.

The Millner Family

According to descendants of the Millner family, their ancestors Abraham (1816-1908) and his twin sons Yosef (Joseph) (1858-1902) and Zundel (John) (1858-1934) joined with Moyshe Herder in New York City. After the failure of Newport, they moved to St. Louis. We know that Zundel became a grocer.

Mr. Spies

Mr. Spies was part of the defunct Sicily Island, Louisiana commune and went with the Herders to try again.

Mr. A. Wiysel

Mr. Alexander Wiysel (1824-?) lived in various parts of the United States. In 1859, he settled in Jacksonport, Arkansas and opened a sawmill and lumber yard.

Woskoboynikoff (Waskoff) Family

They came on the ship the *Bohemia* with the Herders. Mordechai (1853) was only 29 on the voyage and his wife Sheyndel who was 28 (1854). They came with their boys: Hirsch (1874) and Mendel (1878). After the failed Newport, Arkansas colony, they joined the Vineland, New Jersey community and changed their name to Waskoff.

26

Notes

1. A traditional Eastern European water heater for tea that includes a teapot for tea concentrate.
2. The Jewish term for pogroms.
3. A tiny Jewish village
4. German for Mr.
5. German for Miss.
6. Head covering, a shawl or kerchief.
7. German for "Yes, sir!"
8. German for "yes."
9. German for "good."
10. Refers to the Jewish laws regarding the preparation and eating of food.
11. A German language daily labor newspaper
12. Matzah is an unleaved cracker baked specifically for the Passover period. It mimics the unrisen bread the Hebrews took with them when they left ancient Egypt, as described in the Biblical book of Exodus.
13. Russian for yes
14. Russian for good
15. Russian for thank you.

16. Loosely translates from the Hebrew as charity.
17. Loosely translates form the Hebrew as good deed.
18. Hebrew literally meaning, the name. A way of referencing God.
19. Hebrew, for blessed is God.

Printed in the USA
CPSIA information can be obtained
at www.ICGtesting.com
CBHW072006100824
12961CB00027B/1295